Lock Down Publications and Ca$h
Presents

I0664140

Cartel
Money 2
Bricks, Bullets & Blood

Written By
Martell "Troublesome" Bolden

MARTELL "TROUBLESOME" BOLDEN

Lock Down Publications
P.O. Box 944
Stockbridge, GA 30281
www.lockdownpublications.com

Like our page on Facebook: Lock Down Publications
www.facebook.com/lockdownpublications.ldp

Stay Connected with Us!

Text **LOCKDOWN** to 22828 to stay up-to-date with new releases, sneak peaks, contests and more…

Like our page on Facebook:
Lock Down Publications

Join Lock Down Publications/The New Era Reading Group

Visit our website:
www.lockdownpublications.com

Follow us on Instagram:
Lock Down Publications

Email Us: We want to hear from you!

ACKNOWLEDGEMENTS

For those of y'all who don't know me, I did a lot of shit in my life while in the streets that I ain't too proud of. However, neither am I ashamed of the shit I did. Ultimately some of the shit I did landed me in prison for an extensive amount of time. Although, I refuse to allow imprisonment to prevent me from being a dream chaser. I'm locked up physically, not mentally. Feel me.

I ain't the type up of nigga who swap murder stories and/or boast about how much paper I played with in the streets; instead, I speak about it through writing street lit from personal experiences—and at times I tend to make it a l'il more entertainment for y'all, the readers.

Soon, I'll be returning to the streets, then it'll be my turn to get to the bag, go hard for success, and glaze on the naysayers. Shout out to the chosen few who stayed down for the come up; I would say names, but then I'd be snitchin'—and I'ont get down like that. Real spill.

If you care to get in touch with me for any information, input, and/or reviews on my works, then I can be reached via the following avenues.

Postal mailing address:
Martell Bolden #508318
P.O. box 189
Phoenix, MD 21131

Texting/mailing app:
TextBehind.com (Just search his name using this app)

Facebook/Instagram:
Martell Bolden

I 'preciate y'all for supporting a real one.

Chapter 1

Peso was fortunate to have come out on top in the shootout with Salvador. Only he and the three men with him that day knew how close they had come to being the losers. That shootout didn't just cement Peso's reputation; it elevated his aura of invincibility in the streets while simultaneously putting a massive target on his back with law enforcement.

Peso nurtured the image of invincibility with a deft gesture: he cashed out on a bust-down Cuban link necklace with a custom pendant shaped like a target. The pendant wasn't just jewelry—it was a warning to anyone who even thought about aiming for him. But the notoriety came with its drawbacks. To the DEA, Peso was now one of the most infamous drug dealers in Milwaukee. Rightly or wrongly, almost every narcotics seizure in the city was assumed to be connected to Peso. It was one of the prices a kingpin paid for his notoriety.

Even with the heat from the Feds, Peso and his gang kept the money flowing, always staying vigilant.

Seated at a table in Lu's, a local spot they locked down for privacy, Peso held a meeting with his most trusted men. The kingpin had summoned them there. The restaurant was closed—completely empty except for Peso and his crew. Peso sat across from Raul while Chato and Felix occupied the other two chairs, and Paulie stood nearby. These were some of the most trusted members of the gang.

"Paulie, why don't you make us some drinks? Patrón all around," Peso instructed casually, leaning back in his chair. Paulie nodded and headed to the bar.

Peso continued, addressing his men: "I called y'all here to let it be known—I'm finna hit Miami for a couple days, takin' care of some business, and I'm takin' Felix with me. While I'm gone, Raul, it's on you to make sure shit here keeps runnin' smooth."

Paulie returned with the drinks, handing Peso a glass first before serving the others.

"Peso, you go and take care of business out of town, and I'll be sure things here are good," Raul assured him. He took a swig of his drink. "But what about the next load? It should be ready soon."

"It's on you to make sure it touches down," Peso said, locking eyes with Raul. "Once it lands, you gon' handle distribution and collect the paper. All of it." Peso leaned back in his seat.

"Say no more, hombre. I'll handle it, and I'll make sure the money's right," Raul promised confidently.

"Fa sho."

After knocking back a couple drinks, Peso excused himself and headed to the back office. He had some profits to count—money delivered earlier by one of his runners. When his runners came back from a run, it was usually with 40, 50, even 60 racks in cash, stuffed in a beat-up tote bag. Peso had a strict expectation: the money better be stacked neatly by denomination in bundles of five or ten Gs, tied tight with rubber bands. Any sloppy shit—like one-dollar, five-dollar, or even ten-dollar bills—set him off. On busy nights, two or three runners would come in at the same time, and Peso would find himself in an all-night marathon, counting all the lush greenbacks until the sun came up. Once everything was tallied, Peso would stash the money at one of his safe houses.

7

As Peso settled into the desk chair, Raul followed him into the office. Raul had something on his mind—an idea that could make them both more money.

Of all the men in his crew, Raul was the one Peso trusted most. Raul was trusted to take care of miscellaneous drug-related tasks such as escorting shipments and guarding stash houses. After smokin' Ceaser, starting the bloody feud between Peso and Salvador's crews, Raul became Peso's enforcer—a role he played viciously. His body count had earned him respect and fear alike. Raul had killed a number of people at Peso's behest. He sometimes killed on the spur of the moment, in a fit of anger.

Raul's loyalty and body of work earned him a prime position in Peso's operation. By now, Raul had built a small crew of his own, capable of moving large quantities of drugs throughout the city. This newfound leverage made Raul more than just a soldier—he was someone Peso could work with, even depend on.

Peso turned on the money counter, its mechanical hum filling the room. "You coulda talked with me at the table," he said, his eyes fixed on the bundles of cash.

"Figured it would be best that we talk in your office alone," Raul replied. He took a seat on the opposite side of the desk. "Why don't I help you count up the money while we talk?"

Peso leaned back in his chair. "Talk to me."

"Peso, I been handlin' all types of business in this game for you for a while now," Raul began, his tone steady. "And I think it's time you take me on as a business partner."

Peso's brow arched and he gave Raul a hard look. "You think just 'cause you are like my brotha, I should do business with you?"

Raul shook his head. "This has nothin' to do with that. I think you should do business with me 'cause we can be beneficial to each other," he clarified.

Peso leaned forward, his tone skeptical. "How exactly?"

Raul sat upright, his voice calm but assertive. "We can move more product together. Now that I have my own crew of dealers, we can take over more territory. And I'll cop my work through you, so we both make money," he pitched. "You already trust me enough to run the entire operation in your absence. How 'bout it?"

On one hand, he knew Raul had proven himself time and again, running missions, guarding stash houses, and handling business in the streets without breaking stride. On the other hand, making someone a partner in the game came with risks. Still, Peso wasn't blind to the opportunity Raul was laying out.

"Raul," Peso started, his tone deliberate, "I'ont doubt you could run your own operation under me. I'm willin' to take you on as my business partner." He paused, letting the words sink in before continuing, "But you have to pitch in more on the hustle fee. We need that bread to keep the block greased and twelve off our ass. You good with that? "

Raul nodded without hesitation. "I got no problem with that, Peso. Let's make it happen."

Peso grabbed a fat stack of cash from the pile and slapped it onto the desk in front of Raul. "A'ight then. Now, help me count this paper," he said, feeding the first stack of bills into the money counter.

The partnership was official now. Peso and Raul would move weight together, leveraging their combined resources to expand their territory and profits. While Raul had the freedom to work deals independently, he still owed a cut to Peso as the kingpin of the south side—a tax for operating under his established empire. For Peso, it was all about business, and Raul's proposal made sense. They were about to take the hustle to the next level.

Chapter 2

Peso's gang had been growing fast, even before the showdown with Salvador. Branches were springing up throughout the city, and drug dealers from as far away as Michigan, Nebraska, and Arkansas came to Milwaukee to do business with Peso. Buyers sometimes sent their own people to pick up the purchase and traffic it to their states, but more frequently paid extra to have Peso send it to them using his own couriers. Those couriers were often trusted acquaintances from Peso's neighborhood, people like Donnie.

At the Diamond Inn Hotel, a buyer from Detroit named Rip was waiting to meet Peso. This was their first face-to-face meeting, and Peso would let Rip know who was in control.

With a half-dozen of his shooters in tow, Peso pulled up at the hotel. They stepped out of the vehicles and approached Rip's hotel room. As soon as the hotel door opened, the shooters rushed in like commandos and took positions around the room—after checking the bathroom, the closet, and anywhere else someone with sinister intent could hide. Rip remained seated on the couch while his right-hand men stood idle, watching cautiously.

Then Peso walked into the room, looking every bit the Mexican thug who would rather shoot you than talk. Without saying a word, he strode past Rip—who was by then dizzy with fear—and plopped down on the bed. With his pillow against his back and brand-new Air Jordans stretched out on the bedspread, Peso snarled, "Let's talk money."

"I'm lookin' to cop five bricks of boy. Money ain't a problem," Rip cut to the chase, looking at Peso through his Cartier frames.

Rip was a major distributor back in his hometown. He had gotten plugged with Peso through a mutual drug associate. In his early twenties, Rip was a dark-skinned, chubby nigga with a nappy fro and a knack for getting money. The bust-down grill in his mouth, along with his heavy chain and iced-out watch, made it obvious he was eating good in the game.

"I can make that happen for you for a quarter mill'," Peso told him.

"Say no more. Plus, I need it sent to me within a week."

"That'll run you an extra twenty Gs upfront," Peso said, "but I'll make sure you receive the load wherever you want it sent."

"How 'bout' I give you half the paper now, then the other half once the load is delivered?" Rip suggested.

"Give the paper to my nigga." Peso nodded towards Raul. Standing up from the bed, Peso got in Rip's face and said, "Remember this: if anything happens to my runner or the load while in your care, I'ma come with so many steppers to tear your city apart until I find you and make you pay with your life."

Rip nodded emphatically, his confidence visibly shaken as an icy terror gripped his chest and throat.

Once the money was counted out and secured, Peso and his men exited the hotel room. Peso and Raul returned to Peso's BMW 760, with Peso behind the wheel and Raul in the passenger side. They pulled out into traffic with a carload of shooters—including Chato and Paulie—trailing closely behind them. They rolled out to the bass-heavy beat of 42 Dugg's "Dog Food" blasting through the speakers.

Peso pulled out his phone and dialed Felix who was at the stash spot. "Felix," he began once Felix answered, "I need you to get five boys prepared to work." Speaking in coded language just in case the line was tapped, Peso instructed Flex to prepare five keys of heroin for distribution before ending the call.

Raul glanced over at Peso. "Peso, how we don't know if that nigga will try to pull a fast one?"

Peso smirked. "Inspire fear. It's a lesson I learned from my drug-dealin' dad when I was knee-high," Peso replied. "You saw the fear in his eyes. He knows if he don't pay up, I'll come myself to collect his life. That's how you keep niggas in line."

Raul nodded in agreement. "I understand. Fear is the first step to creatin' loyal, easily managed clientele. Now we just gotta get a trusted runner to deliver the load."

"That's where Donnie comes in. I'll send a shooter in a second whip to escort him for protection. First, we need to go and let Donnie know what's up."

Donnie had been running loads for Peso since the day Peso's gunmen murdered Ceaser and seriously wounded his brother, Junior, sparking the bloody feud between Peso's and Salvador's crews. Donnie quickly became an invaluable asset, boosting company profits with his ingenuity. Over time, Donnie perfected a difficult-to-detect smuggling technique that eventually allowed Peso to traffic hundreds of thousands of dollars' worth of drugs—perhaps millions if measured in street value—from and to wherever. The method involved vehicles with false gas tanks and hidden floorboard compartments. It was a way to stay a step ahead of law enforcement.

Peso steered the Beamer toward Donnie's home while Raul texted Donnie.

RAUL:
On the way to your place becuz we need to discuss things.

A moment later, Donnie texted back in reply:

DONNIE:
Not at the crib, so meet up with me at Jalisco's instead.

Raul instructed Peso where to go. Shortly after, the BMW, followed by the sedan, pulled into the restaurant's parking lot. Raul texted Donnie to inform him that they were outside, and it wasn't long before Donnie along with his girlfriend, Toya, emerged from the restaurant. Donnie turned to her and said, "Go wait in the car while I talk with my boys," and Toya did as she was told. Meanwhile, Peso, Raul, and Donnie stood near the Beamer, with shooters posted strategically around them, keeping watch.

"Damn, I see you keep some killas around you," Donnie remarked, taking note of the armed men.

"I'm gettin' more money, so I bought some more killas," Peso replied coolly.

"It's gettin' crazy. L'il by l'il, many people I know are gettin' smoked," Donnie said, shaking his head.

"Donnie, that's just part of the game," Raul chimed in.

"And so is bein' arrested and thrown in jail, but it doesn't make it okay," Donnie shot back. "Look, all I'm sayin' is that sooner or later, I wanna go legit and start myself a landscaping business and get out of drug traffickin' entirely."

"And that's a good thing, Donnie," Peso said, nodding. "I think we all wanna get out the game someday before it's too late. And I'll do my best to help you set up the landscaping business. But that'll take some money. So for now, I'ma pay you ten Gs to run a load."

"Peso, on more than one occasion, I got shot at by someone hopin' to steal the load," Donnie pointed out. Despite his aversion to violence, Donnie could not avoid becoming a target in the game.

"And you had protection, didn't you? That's why I always send a shooter to escort you. Thanks to the armed security, the several hijackin' attempts failed. So don't trip— I'll send Paulie with you on this one. Do you think you can handle it?" Peso asked.

Though all of the violence and killing were beginning to scare him, along with thoughts of getting arrested, Donnie knew it was still far easier to make money in the game than in any legit business. "Peso, I'ma continue runnin' loads for you, but only until I stack up enough money to invest in my business," he said. "Now gimme the details."

"Within the next week, I need you to run a load to a nigga named Rip in Detroit. Then collect a hundred and twenty-five racks of mine. When you get there, call this number," Peso said, texting Rip's cellphone number to Donnie. "If you run into any problems, call me, and I'll handle 'em," Peso told him.

"I'll get in touch with you soon to pick up the load," Donnie said. "Then I'll jump in traffic right away."

Peso pulled a wad of cash out of the pocket of his Palm Angel jeans; he counted out ten bands and paid Donnie in advance. "There's the payment for the run. And here's a loan of five Gs you can put towards your business," he said, and handed over five grand more. The gesture was equal parts generosity and calculated goodwill.

After handling business, Peso n'em parted ways. With Donnie now on board to deliver the load to Rip in Detroit within the next week, all Peso had to do now was get paid the other half of the cost.

As they rode through traffic, Raul glanced at Peso and said, "I understand that you wanna help Donnie with his business and all but remember that loans are meant to be paid back."

"Fuck it," Peso coolly replied, swerving the Beamer around a slow-moving vehicle. "I'm a rich nigga. I'ont expect him to pay me back."

Chapter 3

At the stash house, Raul was posted up with a runner, making sure everything was straight for the next load. It was his responsibility to ensure the shipment arrived safely from Mexico, distribute what was already owed, and collect the funds. As the underboss, Raul was left in charge while Peso was out of town on a business trip, and Raul wasn't about to disappoint him.

"Soon as the load touch down, bring it straight to me," Raul instructed the runner. "I'll handle the distribution myself, 'cause I wanna be sure the money is collected and correct." Raul was the type to stay on top of business—no room for errors.

The runner nodded in agreement, and Raul peeled off five grand from a fat stack of cash as payment for the run. He handed the runner the cash and provided him with one of the vehicles equipped with trap compartments to stash the product. To make sure nothing went sideways, Raul also sent a shooter along for security.

"It'll be on you if anything happens to the load," Raul warned, locking eyes with the runner. His tone was cold, leaving no room for misinterpretation. Once the runner dipped, Raul moved back inside the stash house, pleased he'd had things all taken care of.

As Raul stepped in, his iPhone buzzed in the back pocket of his Amiri jeans. He pulled it out and glanced at its screen. Seeing that the call was from Chato, he answered: "What's up?"

"What's up is while me and Paulie are out here collectin' money from the trap spots like you asked us to, we noticed there's a trap spot in our territory that we don't know shit about," Chato said, sounding heated. "Apparently, whoever's runnin' that trap is gettin' money without dealin' with us," Chato explained dramatically. "What do you want us to do?"

Raul's face hardened. "Just go and try to find out who runs the trap and figure out who they coppin' from. Let 'em know that if they ain't coppin' work from us, then they can't move no work at all," Raul directed.

"Say no more. We on it," Chato responded before ending the call.

Raul slid his phone back into his pocket and dropped down onto the leather couch in the front room. He still had a few more things to tend to before the day was done, but for now, he was finna roll up a blunt and take a moment to relax. Once the blunt was rolled, Raul set flames to the high-grade weed. The rich, pungent smoke filled the air as Raul leaned back, letting the tension melt away. Midway through his blunt, his iPhone buzzed again. This time it was a text from Peso. Raul tapped the screen to open the message.

PESO:
Hope shit is all good with you.
I'll touch down in a few days.

Raul exhaled a thick cloud of smoke and texted back.
RAUL:
Shit good with me.

PESO:
A'ight. Make sure you watch your back.

RAUL:
Fa sho.

After sending the the reply, Raul tossed the phone onto the couch next to him, leaned back in his seat, and took another pull from the blunt, savoring the elation. Being in charge had its perks, but he never let himself forget Peso's position and what it meant. Peso's spot at the top tempted cutthroats and backstabbers. If Raul ever got too comfortable, he knew that'd be the exact moment someone would try to snake him.

Blowing out another plume of smoke, Raul sat deep in thought. For now, he'd hold it down for Peso—but he kept one eye on the money and the other on his back.

Chato chambered a shell in his Glock as he and Paulie, who had his Kel-Tec 9mm tucked in his waistband, pulled the Infiniti striker to the curb in front of the unpermitted trap spot. Chato was there to find out who ran the trap in order to make him understand who ran the territory. He had the temerity to confront whoever was in charge, and he was prepared to pop off.

"Stay on point. If one of them niggas try somethin', don't hesitate to pop his ass," Chato said, his voice firm but low.

"I got'chu," Paulie assured him.

"We gonna go and see who's runnin' this trap and let 'em know what's up." Chato crammed the Glizzy in his waistband. "Let's do this."

Both men stepped out—Chato from the passenger side, Paulie from the driver's—and left the Infiniti running. All eyes were focused in on them as Chato was in step with Paulie heading towards the trap spot where four thuggish-looking niggas were posted on the porch. Chato peeped how two of the young thugs clutched the blicks on their waists while wearing mean mugs. He and Paulie halted on the sidewalk.

One thug, sitting on the porch steps with gold teeth shining, leaned forward aggressively. "Is there a problem or somethin'?"

"Yeah, there is," Chato remarked. "Who runs this H spot?"

"I do," the thug, dark as midnight, replied abrasively, eyeing them sharply.

"Then you the nigga I need to holla at. This is our territory, so anyone movin' work around here have to cop weight from us. Apparently, you ain't coppin' from us, so who you coppin' from?"

Midnight snarled. "It don't matter who I'm coppin' my work from. Nigga, I advise you to move the fuck around with that shit before it gets bad."

With no hesitation, Chato came off the hip, leveling his Glock on Midnight. Instantly, two of the thugs upped their sticks on Chato and Paulie. It had become a tense situation real quick.

"What y'all wanna do?" Chato growled, glaring at Midnight.

"Whatever you wanna do," Midnight tempted.

Paulie tried to defuse the situation: "Chato, let's spare these niggas. We'll catch 'em some other time."

Chato swept his weapon side to side as he and Paulie backpedaled towards the Infiniti. The two thugs held aim on them, but no one fired. As Chato and Paulie started to get inside the Infiniti, the young thugs let off.

Boc-boc-boc-boc-boc!

Boom-boom-boom-boom!

Bullets flew both ways as Chato and Paulie instantly busted back. One of the young thug's spray of bullets hit Chato once in the stomach. Paulie was bustin' over the hood of the Infiniti at Midnight and his thugs with rapid gunfire from his Kel-Tec, forcing them to duck for cover, which gave him and Chato some time to jump into the vehicle. As they sped away from the curb, the thugs began to Swiss-cheese the Infiniti, shattering some windows and flattening a front tire while Chato and Paulie kept their heads low out of the line of fire. Paulie bent a sharp right at the corner, but not having his eyes on the road, due to his head being ducked low, he crashed into a parked car and the Infinity's engine died. "Shit!" Paulie yelled, glancing at Chato, who was clutching his bleeding stomach.

Realizing they couldn't stay, the two bolted from the vehicle, Paulie helping a limping Chato as they fled on foot. By sheer luck, as they darted across a main street, they spotted Donnie at a gas station, just finishing up. Donnie looked up as they approached, seeing Chato clutching his stomach and blood dripping from his hand.

"I need you to gimme a ride to the stash house right now," Chato practically begged.

Donnie sighed, glancing between the bleeding Chato and the panicked Paulie. "I'll give you a ride," Donnie said. "But I'm not gettin' involved in your gunplay. You can get someone else to do that shit for you."

The three men hurriedly climbed into Donnie's Audi SUV. As they sped through traffic, Chato coughed up clumps of blood onto the backseat floor. He groaned in pain, his breathing labored.

"Just breathe, Chato," Paulie urged. "You gonna be a'ight."

"What the fuck happened?" Donnie asked.

"We confronted some niggas about havin' a trap spot in our territory," Paulie explained quickly. "They acted like they didn't give a fuck about us. That's when the shootin' started."

This was just another event that persuaded Donnie it was time to start considering other options and get out of the game. Donnie thought it ironic. He wasn't into violence but those around him were continuously gettin' smoked in ambushes and shootouts. He had seen both Ceaser and Juan succumb to gunfire.

Once they made it to the stash house, Paulie and Donnie helped a weak Chato inside, laying him down on the leather couch in the front room. Raul rushed over as soon as he saw the scene, his face hard with anger.

"Look, I brought him here, but leave me out of it," Donnie said, stepping back. "Call me when there's a load to run." He turned for the front door, wanting no part of what came next.

"Later, Donnie," Raul called after him. He turned his attention to the matter at hand. "Paulie, let's get Chato into the car and take him to the hospital."

Raul's blood boiled as he assessed Chato's injuries. This happened on his watch, and now he had to report to Peso that his younger cousin had been shot. By any means necessary, Raul vowed to retaliate. Someone was going to pay for this.

***

The Miami sun seemed to sink into the Atlantic Ocean as it set, painting the sky a deep burnt orange, creating a stunning backdrop. Back in Milwaukee, there was a cold breeze and littered streets, but Miami was a whole different vibe—sunshine, sandy beaches, palm trees swaying in the winds, and boats bobbing on the ocean waves.

At a Colombian eatery on the main strip, Manuel and Peso occupied a table on the outside patio. The meeting was intentional—Manuel felt it necessary to meet with Peso face-to-face so they could gain an understanding. It was apparent that Manuel was a well-respected figure. Many people went out of their way to greet him, and Manuel acknowledged them with polite nods and a suave demeanor before introducing his company. If nothing else, Manuel was a smooth criminal.

Taking a swig from his glass of Patrón, Manuel eyed Peso over the rim of his glass. "Good to see you again, Peso."

"I'd like to visit more often, but I have a lot goin' on back home," Peso replied, his tone casual but weighted. He hadn't been to Miami for a while, especially after avoiding Ceaser's funeral.

"And I imagine whatever you have going on has to do with your people getting shot," Manuel said, referencing the phone call he'd overheard Peso having earlier with Raul about Chato's hospitalization after catching a bullet.

"Actually, it does," Peso admitted to the Colombian, cutting straight to the point. "When you on top, it seems like everyone wanna come for your position."

Manuel swirled his drink in the glass before taking another sip. "I admire that you're willing to do whatever it takes to remain on top."

Peso's gaze hardened, determination flickering in his eyes. "I just know how it feels to climb from the bottom. I'ont ever wanna fall off again."

Manuel reached across the table, placing a reassuring hand on Peso's shoulder. "No need to worry about that. Our arrangement is more than enough to keep you on top. I trust in you, and so do my associates. In fact, instead of sticking to just our original arrangement, I'd like to offer you twenty kilos upfront due to the delay. Unfortunately, the authorities have been disrupting our cocaine suppliers from Colombia. But their efforts won't stop a damn thing. So, are you for it?"

Peso leaned back slightly, confidence in his tone. "Manuel, I'm all for it. I'm already runnin' my operation back home. And I'd like for us to do as much business together as we can."

"I too will like that," Manuel said. "Well, since you're in Miami, how about we have a night on the town? On me."

Chapter 4

The word in the streets Peso picked up was that Greedy was behind his younger cousin Chato getting popped. Turns out, it was actually Greedy's younger cousin Polo who had pulled the trigger.

Adding insult to injury, Greedy had not yet paid for the last brick of heroin Peso fronted him. Instead, he boasted openly about getting away with it—and about Chato being shot—all while live on Instagram. Peso knew he had to make an example out of them. If he wanted to maintain his position in the game and not appear weak, Greedy and Polo had to pay with their lives.

It was night outside when the glacier-white Dodge Challenger SRT slid to the curb in front of the trap spot, with Paulie behind the steering wheel and Raul riding shotgun. It was the very spot where Chato had gotten popped.

"I'ma make this shit quick," Raul said, clutching an AR-15. "If I ain't back in two minutes, then you come in bustin'."

"Say no more," Paulie told him.

Stepping out of the whip, Raul walked towards the trap spot, his weapon ready for action. When he reached the house, he kicked in the front door with authority, barging in with the AR-15 leveled.

Rrraa!

The first guy, who was shot in the forehead, had been standing near the door when Raul burst into the front room, bustin'. The shot caused the guy to do an ungraceful pirouette as he fell to the floor. The other man scrambled for cover between the couch and coffee table. Raul stepped up and stood over him.

"Where's Greedy?" Raul barked, aiming the assault rifle down at his defenseless victim.

"I-I don't know. If I did, I promise I would tell you," the man whimpered. "P-please don't kill me."

"Shut the fuck up!" Raul growled. He fired a round into the back of the man's head, leaving him sprawled dead, face down on the floor.

After the double slaying in the trap spot, Raul rushed out and jumped into the Challenger. Paulie hit the gas, speeding away down the block.

"Pull over right there," Raul instructed Paulie, pointing at a dimly lit side street. "Soon as you hear shots, just pull up on me."

"I got'chu," Paulie assured.

Raul exited the car, gripping the AR-15 tightly. He skulked towards the front street on 6th and Beecher Street, where Greedy was known to frequent. A gang of four dope boys were posted on the block, servin' dope fiends under the flickering glow of a streetlight. Raul stalked towards them, his weapon leveled on the unsuspecting gang.

One of the dope boys peeped the shadow figure creeping up and squinted, "Who the fuck is that?" he asked, reaching for the Glock on his waist as shots erupted from Raul's AR-15.

Rrraa, rrraaa!

Boc, boc!

Once Raul started bustin', the dope boy attempted to bust back but his shots missed and he was instead shot in the ribcage, piercing a lung. He fell to the sidewalk, coughing blood and fumbling his Glock, while the others scattered like roaches. As the wounded dope boy tried crawling away, Raul calmly walked up on him, using his boot to roll him onto his back. "Look at me," Raul demanded, aiming the Ar-15 at the boy's chest. "Tell me, where the fuck can I find Greedy?" Raul hissed.

"You can . . . f-find him at . . . Benny's Pizza," the dope boy managed to tell him as he gasped for air. "I-I . . . told you wh-what you wanna know. Now l-let me live. Please." Raul smirked. "Fuck you."

Rraa!

Several bullets tore through the boy's chest, leaving his body limp and riddled with holes. Raul turned without a shred of remorse and hopped into the Challenger just as Paulie pulled up after hearing the shots. Paulie floored the gas, the tires screeching as they sped away from the carnage.

As they weaved through the streets, Raul barked, "Take me to Benny's Pizza. It's time to handle Greedy's bitch-ass."

***

Benny's Pizza was located at 11th and Lincoln Street, the glowing neon sign lighting up the night. Inside, the pizzeria was packed, customers buzzing around the tables, the smell of fresh pies hanging in the air. Raul and Paulie rolled up in the glacier-white Dodge Challenger SRT, parking out front with a clear view of the action. Through the glass window, they could see Greedy sitting in a booth with two men—one of them instantly recognizable to Paulie. It was Polo, the same nigga from the trap spot during the shootout.

"Let's smoke these niggas without harmin' any innocent bystanders," Raul instructed coldly, his tone sharp with intent. All he wanted was Greedy and his clansmen.

Paulie double-checked his Glock 19, making sure the thirty-shot stick was locked and loaded. "Just leave the dark-skinned nigga to me," he said grimly. He had plans to make Polo feel every bit of the heat he was bringing.

The two shooters pulled on their black Pooh Shiesty masks before stepping out of the Challenger. Their weapons were out in plain sight, glinting under the streetlights. Raul's

AR-15 was slung low, steady, and ready to bark. As they approached the entrance, Raul spotted a young woman with her two kids about to walk in. He threw up a hand to stop them.

"Y'all don't want this," Raul said, nodding at the big gun in his grip.

The mother took one look at the steel and scrambled away with her kids, clutching them tight. Raul and Paulie pushed through the pizzeria doors like death walking in broad daylight. All eyes in the room locked on them, but Raul and Paulie had their sights fixed on the booth where Greedy, Polo, and the third man sat frozen in fear. The three of them looked like they had just seen the Grim Reaper.

Rrraa, rrraaa, rrraaa!

Boom, boom, boom, boom!

The gunfire erupted, tearing through the air, louder than the screams of the fleeing customers. Bullets ripped into their targets before any of the three had a chance to reach for their weapons. . Greedy was hit multiple times, one shot tearing through his neck. Blood sprayed across his diamond-flooded Cuban link, dripping like crimson paint. Polo, who was popped in the face and chest, tried to muster up strength to go for his gun until Paulie stuck the barrel of the Glock to his eye and blew his noodles out.

Meanwhile, the third man didn't even get a chance to twitch. A single bullet pierced his heart, and he slumped forward onto the table, his face landing square in a greasy pepperoni pizza.

Raul and Paulie hurried out of the pizzeria.

Innocent bystanders hit the floor during the shooting, some diving under tables, others hugging the ground to avoid stray bullets. Panic spread like wildfire. Once the shots stopped and the sound of footsteps faded, the brave few cautiously rose from their hiding spots. What they found was a scene straight out of hell: three bodies laid out in blood, one slumped over a pizza, their killers vanished into the night.

Chapter 5

Many of South Side residents sighed with a relief when Salvador was killed, thinking the violence might finally end now that Peso's arch-rival was out of the way.

But the murders continued. New adversaries emerged, and old scores still needed settling. Bodies continued turning up in alleyways, sometimes with faces gnawed away by rats.

For the people of the South Side, the only consolation was that the hoodlums seemed to be taking each other out. At least innocent citizens weren't caught in the crossfire. Once returning from his business trip, Peso made his way to go visit his younger cousin, Chato, in the hospital. He was grateful Chato had survived the near-fatal gunshot wound that left him needing surgery and forced to wear a colostomy bag. But Peso had already ensured the assailants got hit like Chato got hit, but they ain't fuckin' breathing to tell the tale.

Entering Chato's hospital room, Peso was trailed by Raul, Felix, and Paulie. It was the first time any of them had seen Chato since the shooting a few days prior. Chato lay in the hospital bed, hooked up to tubes and machines. Despite the situation, he was thrilled to see Peso n'em.

Peso stepped to Chato's bedside, dapped him up and said, "Good to see you, l'il cuz. How you feelin'?"

"Lucky to still be alive," Chato admitted.

"Well, them other chochas can't say the same." Peso smirked.

"No doubt. Wish I was there to see 'em drop."

Raul piped up, "Believe me, we made sure they dropped dead. Ain't that right, Paulie?"

"Fa sho. And I personally dropped the one who popped you," Paulie added with a nod.

A smirk spread across Chato's lips as he imagined the retaliation. "That's what's up."

"Ain't no way in hell were we gonna let Greedy get away with tryin' to finesse Peso or his people get away with poppin' you," Felix chimed in.

"That's just another message for niggas to know not to come for us," Peso said.

The others nodded in agreement, though they all understood it did not mean old or new rivals would not come for them.

Chato begun to sit up, but he winced in pain. "Ah, shit," he hissed, grimacing. He was still sore from the operation on the colon to make an artificial anus in his abdominal wall.

"You a'ight, l'il cuz?" Peso asked out of concern as he assisted Chato in sitting up.

"Yeah. I'm a'ight. Just hate that I gotta wear this shit bag for now and be stuck in this damn hospital."

"It's better than a body bag," Felix commented.

"Facts," Paulie agreed.

"They're right, Chato," said Raul.

Peso planted a reassuring hand on his younger cousin's shoulder. "Just rest up for now. Soon, you'll be back in the field with us."

After all of them said their parting words to Chato, they left the hospital. Once the gang made it outside, where the air was biting cold, they loaded into Raul's Range Rover. The vehicle's speakers blasted EST Gee's track "More Blood" As they rode, Peso asked to be dropped off at home.

During the ride, Peso's mind was focused on Chato. Deep down he faulted himself for his younger cousin's life even in danger. Then again, Peso knew Chato understood what he was signing up for when he decided to join the cause.

Shortly after, the Range slid to the curb in front of Peso's place. Before exiting the whip, he dapped up all his boys and told them he would be in touch. As Peso walked towards his place, the Range pulled off, disappearing down the street.

Peso entered the house and removed his Moncler jacket, hanging it neatly on the coat rack near the front door. He checked his daughter's room, expecting to find her sound asleep, but her bed was still made and empty. As he made his way through the living room, he called out for Mona only to receive no response. Confused, he called out, "Mona!" as he moved through the living room, but there was no response. He knew she had to be there—her car was parked outside.

When he stepped into their master bedroom, he noticed steam wafting from beneath the bathroom door and heard the shower running. Pushing the door open, he found Mona bathing herself in the walk-in shower.

"Mona, didn't you hear me callin' your ass?" Peso frustratedly said.

"If I did, then I would have answered you, Lupe," Mona replied, turning to look at him through the glass.

"Well, I could have been anybody walkin' in here. You need to be on point."

Mona grabbed her iPad off the shelf and showed him the camera views from their surveillance footage. "I saw you come in. Pleased now?" she asked, her tone laced with calm sarcasm.

"Yeah, I guess," he gruffed. "And where's Max?"

"She's at your mother's for the night. Tamera wanted to keep her," Mona answered. She could read that he had something else on his mind that had him testy. She paused washing herself, looked to him and said, "Is everything alright? You seem bothered."

"My bad if I come off that way," Peso apologized. He took a seat on the lidded toilet and exhaled. "I just came from seein' my l'il cousin in the hospital, and it was hard on me to

CARTEL MONEY 2

see him that way. Fortunately, he survived . . . but what if he hadn't? I guess I feel like it's my fault he nearly lost his life."

"You can't blame yourself for that, Lupe," Mona said gently. "Chato chose this life. He knew the risks when he got involved. It's not your fault. It just comes with the game," she expressed.

Peso nodded slowly. "You're right, Mona. I guess I'm just tired of losin' people close to me."

"I get it," she said, her voice softening further. "But you'll never have to worry about losing me. Now, why don't you come here and let me show you just how much I don't want to lose you either?" She seductively motioned him toward her with a manicured finger.

Without hesitation, Peso stood. He removed his Glock from his waistband and set it on the toilet lid before kicking off his VaporMax sneakers and pulling off his Nike joggers. His eyes lingered on Mona as she teasingly traced her fingers across her pussy, enticing him further.

After stripping himself nude, Peso then stepped into the walk-in shower, and the warm water rained down on him while he greedily kissed Mona and held her close. His shower of kisses trailed down her neck and over her collarbone until his full lips reached her pretty titties. Peso flicked his long, thick tongue rapidly over one of her erect nipples as he caressed the other between his fingers. Mona gently bit down on her lower lip, enjoying the sensation of her nipples being pleasured. He pushed her back against the wall and lifted her by the ass while she held on to his shoulders. Then Peso guided his enlarged dick deep inside of Mona's slippery pussy.

Peso grunted as he thrust his hips back and forth, sliding his dick in and out of her pussy. "Mona, this pussy so good, boo." She gasped softly in his ear and he enjoyed knowing that he was taking her breath away. Peso sped up his thrusts, wanting to make her reach climax. "Cum for me, bae. Cum for me."

29

"Dammit, Lupe! Don't stop until I cum all over your dick!" Mona moaned. She gripped his shoulders tight, digging her almond-shaped manicure nails into his flesh. "Oh, my goodness, you're hitting my spot!" Her moans loudly echoed within the steamy bathroom as Peso pounded away at her twat. It wasn't long before Mona came: "Oooooh, yeeeessss!"

Peso felt her warm cum coat his dick. He planted her onto her pedicured feet and kissed her passionately as they shared tongues. Mona gripped his hardness in her petite hand and began gently stroking it. She lowered onto her knees, then flicked her pierced tongue rapidly over the swollen tip of Peso's dick while gazing up into his eyes. It turned him on to watch her loving him with her sexy mouth as water rained down on them. Mona wrapped her lips firmly around the dick and began bobbing her head back and forth, allowing it to slide deep into the back of her throat.

"Mmmm . . . You like that? Mmmmm . . . It tastes so good," Mona said so seductively in between sucking the dick.

Peso ran his fingers through her wet, long hair, then gripped the back of her head and encouraged her to suck his dick vigorously. "Damn, baby girl, I like that shit so fuckin' much!" he groaned as her lips pleased him. He began fuckin' her mouth, thrusting his hips back and forth. After several minutes of Mona performing on his dick, Peso felt a nut building, then he pulled out of her mouth and released on her pretty face. "Oh, shit!"

The couple stepped out of the shower, then Peso bent Mona over the sink and fucked her from the back. They locked eyes through the huge mirror above the sink. He enjoyed seeing her fuck faces, which made him fuck her even harder, causing their flesh to clap with each thrust. Mona tossed her head back with her mouth open and eyes rolling into the back of her skull as she took the dick. Peso pulled her long hair with one hand while he steadied her juicy ass with his other as he dug her out. They both moaned and groaned from sexual pleasure. Peso turned her around to face him and sat her on the counter of the sink. He slipped his dick inside of her pussy and stroked her while they kissed and she wrapped her arms around the nape of his neck.

"Bae, this wet shit got a nigga about to nut," Peso grunted. He hit the pussy until he busted a nut. Then he knelt between her legs while she remained seated on the sink; he tasted her pussy.

"Uhhh . . . Yes, Lupe, yes . . ." Mona uttered as he licked all over her clit and pussy lips. She held her legs wide open, allowing Peso full access to her honeypot. He paid attention to her clit, sucking and teasing it. "Ahhh . . . I'm cumin', Lupe. I'm cummmin'!" As she had an orgasm, he slurped her juices and cleaned her pussy.

Peso rose to his feet and tongued her down, allowing her to taste her own juices. He said: "Now let's use the shower for what it's actually for."

The couple returned into the shower and helped wash each other clean. But no matter how much soap Peso used, one thing was certain—he could not wash away his bloodstained soul.

***

The Ford F-150 sat parked on a shadowed side street, tucked away in darkness where prying eyes were unlikely to linger.

Captain Danielson occupied the truck, having chosen the secluded spot for his regular meeting with Peso to collect his monthly hustle fee. Moments later, he noticed the Range Rover swerve to the curb and park in front of his truck. Danielson exited the Ford, scanning his surroundings to be sure no one was watching him deal with the kingpin, before slipping into the backseat of the Range.

"How's things going?" Danielson began.

"Things are goin' good," Peso replied from the passenger seat. He observed the crooked cop through the rearview mirror.

Danielson scoffed and leaned forward slightly. "You mean besides all of the damn shootings lately that are related to a drug war? Peso, there's a lot being put on your name. Your notoriety is doing more than putting a target on your back. Other big-time dealers are using it to their advantage, telling their runners to claim loads belong to you if they're caught. Meanwhile, every violent act that happens is automatically being pinned on you. Whether it's yours or not, every bullet fired, every body dropped, they're saying it's Peso's work. You're starting to look downright bloodthirsty, and that ain't good for business."

Law enforcement on the north side was growing increasingly concerned about the spike in drug violence, especially since it had begun spilling over to their jurisdiction. Adding to law enforcement worries was the fact that it was just a matter of time before the streets would become uncontrollable battlegrounds.

"Cap, I only retaliate on those who come at me first. I can't control anything else that takes place," Peso firmly replied. He tossed a wad of cash into the captain's lap. "There's your monthly fee. Just keep the Drug Task Force off my operation."

"Alright. Just try to keep a low profile." Captain Danielson pocketed the cash before exiting the Range Rover. Part of him knew that Peso was beginning to get too big, too fast—a storm waiting to break.

Inside the car, Raul pulled off from the curb, sailing through the quiet street. Peso scoffed and shook his head as he watched the crooked cop retreat to the F-150. "It's a damn disgrace," he muttered under his breath. "A man in a position like his, lowering himself so shamefully."

The hypocrisy of the whole arrangement didn't escape Peso. On one hand, he relied on the captain and the Drug

Task Force (DTF) to turn a blind eye to his drug operation, to warn him when raids were coming, and to keep him ahead of the game. On the other hand, even he found their behavior repulsive. But Peso understood the game—every man had a price. And Danielson, for all his self-righteousness, was no different.

Chapter 6

Peso, Raul, Felix, Paulie, and some others were holding a meeting about the upcoming cocaine shipment. They were inside Felix's apartment located on 16th and Cesar Chavez Street. Peso had called them together to update them on his new line of business with the Colombians.

"Now that I'm doing business with the Colombians, there will be more product to be moved," Peso was saying. He was sitting on the couch with a quarter kilo of cocaine on the coffee table in front of him. "Not only will we be movin' heroin and marijuana, but now we'll be pushin' coke too. That said, I need y'all to start linin' up clientele so once the first shipment comes in, then we can have it moved in no time."

"Peso," Raul chimed in. "How much coke are you talkin'? Five, ten keys?"

"Twenty keys to start," Peso replied. "And if we can get it sold and pay back the Colombians ASAP, then there's more where that comes from."

"You trust the Colombians are good for business?" Chato asked skeptically, always cautious.

Peso leaned back in his seat. "If they prove to be bad for business in any way, then I'll cut 'em off like a machete. Until then, it's nothin' personal—just business."

Peso used his pinky nail to scoop substance small bump of coke from the pile of coke, then lifted it to his nostril and tooted the cocaine. Offering the rest to the group, everyone indulged except Paulie. The coke was pure, straight from the steamy, snake-infested jungles of South America.

Once the meeting was adjourned, Peso, Chato, and Paulie left Felix's apartment. It was around midnight and freezing air bit at their skin as they got into the Ford Bronco Wildtrak parked out front. Peso slid behind the steering wheel, Chato rode shotgun, and Paulie occupied the backseat.

Suddenly, a Dodge Journey SE careened out of the shadows. Its occupants leaned out of the windows and started bustin'.

Prrrat, prrrat, prrrat!

Boc, boc, boc, boc, boc!

As Peso sped off, Chato and Paulie busted back at the truck. The truck was on their tail until Peso bent a few corners and shook it. Heads on a swivel, the men scanned their surroundings for any signs of pursuit.

At the busy intersection of 16th and National Street, a Popeye's restaurant sat on one corner, with cars constantly driving in and out of the lot. The traffic light turned red, forcing Peso to stop. That's when it happened—a carefully orchestrated ambush. At least a dozen shooters in multiple vehicles had been lying in wait. The moment the Bronco stopped, they unleashed a barrage of automatic gunfire.

Rrraa, rrraaa, rrraaa!

Ack, ack, ack, ack, ack, ack!

All that spared Peso from instant death was the fact that two working men in a Chevy Traverse happened to drive into the middle of the intersection the instant the shooting began. They were about to turn into the Popeye's parking lot and were hit in the initial fusillade. That gave Peso and his comrades enough time to jump out and take cover between their vehicle and that of the two working men, who were slumped over and covered with blood. The two unlucky working men who'd been caught in the crossfire had been hit repeatedly in the hand, chest, legs, and heads.

Inside of Popeye's, the cashier and customers dropped to the floor or ducked behind counters and under tables as bullets tore into the restaurant's facade and sprayed through the windows into the restaurant. Vehicles that had been approaching the intersection spun around and vanished in a roar down side streets. Peso was shouting for reinforcements into his iPhone. In less than a minute, Felix skidded to a halt nearby, then he and several shooters jumped out of their SUVs and joined the shootout, rifles blazing.

At one point, Peso turned his .45 on a Subaru Impreza backing out of a parking lot stall directly in front of the fast-food restaurant, thinking it was another carload of shooters. When bullets tore through the sheet metal and hit one of the four young men in the foot, the driver frantically backed out to try to get away. That's when Peso opened fire, hitting the Subaru seventeen times. Felix chased them and shot out one of the tires, but the terrified youths abandoned the car, fled on foot, and escaped down a resident street.

Though outnumbered, Peso and his boys were battle-hardened and had steadier nerves than their attackers. These attackers appeared to be young and inexperienced because they were aiming high. One by one, the assailants were shot down. Soon, the only remaining gunmen were holed up inside or behind a Nissan GT-R50.

"Let's finish this!" Peso growled. He, Chato, and Paulie jumped into their Bronco and launched a frontal assault at the men. Braving the bullets, Peso raced through the intersection and sped straight for the Nissan, an audacious counterattack that allowed Peso and his boys to shoot down the last of the assailants.

As they sped away from the massacre, Peso exhaled, his adrenaline still pumping. "I'ont know how many of 'em we killed, but I know we hit a lot of 'em," Peso told his boys as he continued to speed away from the scene of the massacre.

"Who the fuck sent all those shooters?" Paulie questioned.

"Could be some of Greedy's people tryin' to retaliate," Chato rationalized.

Peso shook his head, his mind racing. To him, the ambush had Salvador markings—young, inexperienced shooters. "Naw. I'm sure Junior's behind it. He wants revenge for the death of his dad, his mom, and his brother Ceaser."

"How can you be so sure?" Chato asked.

"Who else could it be?" Peso replied firmly. His jaw tightened as he made up his mind. "We have to find those guys who ran away and make them talk. We need to find out if Junior's behind the ambush or not."

***

Peso had unleashed a furious inquisition to uncover who was behind the Popeye's ambush. He was sure Junior, Ceaser's brother and Salvador's last surviving son, was behind it.

For the following week, machine-gun fire erupted across the south side of town almost every night. No one with even the faintest knowledge of the ambush was spared Peso's scrutiny. A week after the ambush, Peso finally got a lead on one of the young men who had fled on foot. Armed with this information, he decided to pay the family a visit to get answers.

The residents of the house were startled awake well past midnight by a furious banging on their backdoor. A matronly woman with kind eyes and streaks of gray in her hair hastily threw on a robe and leaned her head against the door.

"Who is it?" she asked timidly.

"Open up!" a voice barked from the other side.

There was absolutely no reason for anyone to be banging on the door at their home at three in the morning. They were known in the neighborhood as God-loving people and mindful of the law. And even though there was someone there, shouldn't they have knocked on the front door?

"You can't be anyone we know," the woman said through the door.

The banging started over again. "Open up, goddammit, or we'll shoot the fuckin' door down!"

By then, her husband Julio had gotten up and slipped on trousers and a shirt. He walked to the backdoor in his bare feet and saw the worried expression etched on his wife's face. He opened the door.

It was nearing winter and it was freezing outside. Milwaukee winters were the flip side of the summers: unbearably cold. Julio recognized Peso. Behind him were a dozen men armed with machine guns. Peso held a Draco in his hand, its barrel pointing downward but no less menacing. The husband stepped out into the concrete patio of the backyard and felt the cold through his thin shirt and bare feet.

Peso's voice was menacing. "I know that your son Javier was in a Nissan in front of the Popeye's where the ambush took place. Why didn't you notify the police about the shootin'?" he demanded.

"We were afraid to. We're afraid to tell the police anything," Julio admitted.

"Where's your son?"

"He's sleeping."

"Then wake him the fuck up!"

Julio hesitated.

"Move, goddammit, or I'll wake his ass up myself!" Peso ordered.

Filled with panic, the mother went to rouse her son. But the boy had been awakened by the noise and was hurriedly putting his jogger pants on. She heard a voice that was not Peso's shouting from the backdoor, "Make it fast!"

The mother was a humble woman, a member of Jehovah's Witnesses, as were her husband and son. She believed fervently that there was good in everyone. She told her son: "Don't worry, they won't hurt you. They just want to talk to you."

Once back at the door, she spoke in a quivering voice. "We're not bad people. We don't have any weapons . . . we don't have anything to do with bad people."

"You're comin' with us," Peso told the husband and son, disregarding the wife's pleas.

The house was completely surrounded. Armed men were standing everywhere, and there were five dark-colored vehicles in the street. As they walked to the front of the house, the father recognized one of his neighbors standing to one side, his eyes cast down. The neighbor had been abducted from his home by the dealers who threatened to kill him if he didn't point out the house.

After pushing the two terrified men into one of the vehicles, the dealers blindfolded them and sped out of the neighborhood. They were taking the men to an abandoned building. Soon after, the car stopped in front of the building, and the young man and his father were pulled from the vehicle and pushed inside the abandoned building.

Once inside, they heard the voice of Peso order: "Get 'em ready!"

Father and son were put into separate rooms. The dealers wrapped towels around their heads and secured the towels with bailing wire. Their hands were tied behind with bailing wire too. They were pushed to the ground and forced to lie on their backs. Their captors kicked them in the sides and hit them with rifle butts. Though unable to see, Javier realized from the voice that Peso was doing the interrogating. After questioning the father, Peso went to the son to see if there were any discrepancies.

The worst of the beating was reserved for the son. Peso kept grilling him. "Why were you at Popeye's that night? Why did you shoot at us? Who paid you to try to kill me?"

"It wasn't me, I swear!" the young man cried. Each time he declared innocence, he was showered with punches and kicks.

"Then what were you doin' there the night of the shootout?"

"I drove up to the restaurant with some friends to buy something to eat; we had been cruising around that night. We came out of the restaurant and got into the car just as the shooting started. Of course we ran off. Who wouldn't? Someone was shooting at us for no reason and bullets were coming right through the car," the young man told the interrogators.

Then Peso was back with the father, he threw out dozens of names and asked the older man questions about each one of them. Peso asked him about people on 16th and Arthur Street. A gang of Latin Kings that operated on the south side. "They sent you, didn't they?" he snarled.

"No, they didn't send us to kill you. No one sent us, please believe me," the father pleaded.

Then more questions, more beatings, more savagery. The brutality lasted for three hours. Each time the inquisitors came back into the room, the father begged Peso to spare his son, the son begged Peso to spare his father, their voices breaking under the weight of pain and fear.

In a hallway Peso was with Raul and some others. They were tired of interrogating the men.

"Peso, I'ont think they had anything to do with it," Raul told him.

"I need to know who did it," Peso replied. "I'm certain Junior was behind it. Who else could it be?"

"Well, apparently these two don't know a damn thing."

Finally, Peso ordered: "Get 'em outta here."

The two men were lifted to their feet, taken outside and pushed into a vehicle. The towel blindfolds were still wrapped tightly around their heads. Their hands were still bound behind their backs. The vehicle rolled over potholes in the streets, and it was difficult for them to keep upright. The older man wondered if they were being taken someplace to be shot in back of the head.

Ten minutes after they had been shoved into the vehicle, it stopped. A voice snapped, "Get the fuck out, and make it fast."

They did as they were told, trembling. Except for the idling of the motor, all was silent outside. And bitterly cold. The older man was still barefoot. The muscles of his neck and upper back stiffened involuntarily. Any second now, he thought, a bullet would crash into the back of his head. He wanted to touch his son one last time, but his hands were bound too tightly.

Then he heard a motor rev up. The vehicle drove away. It drove farther and farther away until he could not hear it anymore. The younger man managed to work his own hands free, then ripped the towels off his father's head and untied his hands.

Rubbing their eyes and looking around in the darkness, the father and son realized they were only a few blocks away from home.

Peso never found out for sure who was behind the ambush. At one point, he thought the attempt on his life might have been the work of the Latin Kings from 16th and Arthur Street, believing they wanted to install their own man as kingpin of the south side, but his investigation eventually ruled out them out. Peso became convinced Junior had hired a dozen shooters to kill him in revenge for the deaths of his father, mother, and brother. Junior's mistake was hiring young, inexperienced shooters, and so the attempt had failed—just as Salvador's earlier ambush at Lu's Restaurant had failed.

Peso's resolve hardened. "I'm gonna make Junior pay," he vowed.

Chapter 7

Following Donnie's run to Detroit, he stopped by Lu's to see Peso. Donnie had successfully delivered the bricks of boy to Rip and collected the money owed to Peso without any problems. All that was left was for him to drop the money off to Peso and wrap up the job.

Entering Lu's, Donnie noticed, as usual, Peso shooters lounging around the place, with their artillery on display. He saw Chato and approached him. "How're you, Chato?" he greeted.

"I'm alive," Chato replied.

"For a nigga who just took a bullet, you out here."

Chato scoffed. "Bullet wounds are part of the street life. Anyways, wassup?"

"Where's Peso? I need to see him."

"He's in the back office. C'mon." Chato led Donnie to the office in the back and tapped on the door.

"It's open," Peso called out. Chato pushed open the door, and Donnie entered. Chato closed the door before heading away. Peso was seated behind the desk, and he motioned for Donnie to take a seat across from him.

"Here's the money from the Detroit run." Donnie set a tote bag on the desk. "I counted it myself; it's all there."

Peso pulled the bag closer, unzipped it, and checked the neatly stacked cash inside. "Good lookin' on makin' the run. Hope it wasn't too much trouble for you."

"None at all. And it was easy and worth the money," Donnie said. "By the way, I 'preciate you borrowin' me the extra money towards my business."

"Don't even mention it."

"Well, just let me know if there's anything else you need for me to do for you."

"Actually, there is," Peso said as he stood from his seat. He made his way around the desk, then perched on edge of it. "I have fifty Gs if you kidnap Junior and bring him to me," he offered.

Donnie stood, his tone firm. "Peso, let me make somethin' clear: I'ont want any part in violence," he told Peso. "I'll do anything you want me to do, with one exception. Don't ask me to kill anybody. I'ont want any part of it." What Peso didn't know was that just after Salvador's death, Junior had offered Donnie money to kill Peso—an offer Donnie had also declined.

"Donnie, you're the one who's in need of money to leave the game and go legit," Peso pointed out.

"I understand. But there are other ways for me to make money. I have no problem makin' runs until I make enough money to get out of the game. So if you need me to make more runs for you, then I'm in."

"I feel you. Just know that my offer will remain on the table in case you decide to change your mind," Peso said.

"Trust me, I won't," Donnie assured. He just was not about to get in the middle of the beef. "Just get at me when you need me to run a load." He dapped Peso before making his way out.

Peso understood Donnie's position and respected it. He resolved not to approach Donnie about violent matters again. However, Peso still needed to find a way to get Junior before Junior could get him. And with Junior being so damn vigilant, it would not be easy for Peso to get close to him. Therefore, Peso would have to strike at the right time and place, then take him out.

***

While Donnie lay in bed beside his girl, Toya, the two breathed heavily after having sex. Donnie loved Toya, although their relationship was far from perfect. Over the years, Toya had caught Donnie cheating, and after one particularly bad fight where he put his hands on her, she left him. Yet, she had returned on more than one occasion. Despite knowing they weren't a good match, Toya had to admit she loved Donnie, and they kept trying for the sake of their child. Donnie grabbed a partially smoked blunt out of the ashtray on the nightstand and sparked it up. "I spoke with Peso the other day and told him that I won't be runnin' loads for him once I stack enough cash to go legit," he said, then puffed the blunt. "I just wanna get outta the game before it's too late."

After seeing so many either go to prison or be murdered, Donnie was growing concerned. Not only for himself, but for Toya as well. Toya was down for him and hustled with him, so Donnie wanted to make sure she was safe.

Suddenly, Donnie's iPhone rang. He reached over, grabbed the phone, and checked its screen. He noticed that the caller was a woman everybody knew as TT. She was the wife of one of Peso's father's close friends, Oscar, who had recently been arrested by DEA for marijuana trafficking. Oscar had ran a crew of dealers supplied by Peso. After Oscar's arrest, TT continued to handle her husband's operation.

Donnie answered, "Wassup?"

"I need your help," TT replied.

"With what?"

"Why don't you drop by my place so we can talk in person?"

"A'ight, TT, I'll be there in a l'il bit."

Donnie ended the call. He stepped out of bed and got dressed, then headed out to his car in order to go and meet with TT. About half an hour later, Donnie had arrived at TT's place. She invited him inside, and they sat down on the couch in the front room.

Puffing on a cigarette, TT got straight to the point. "I have close to twenty pounds of marijuana that I need to have smuggled to Minnesota."

"Why didn't you just have someone else do it?" Donnie asked.

"I'm counting on you, because I know if you take it, it will get there safely and I won't get robbed," she explained.

Donnie was trying to get out of the running business but he had to make some runs in order to stack enough money to do so. "How much are you willin' to pay me?"

"Five grand. But I need the load shipped out immediately."

"Where's the load now?"

"It's here. Follow me."

TT led Donnie out the back door and into the garage behind her home. The moment they stepped in, the pungent smell of marijuana hit Donnie's nose. It was a familiar smell.. TT stepped over to a box and opened it for Donnie to see its contents. Donnie inspected the marijuana, shaking his head as he realized something. He had learned to tell the differences. This stuff was exactly like the weed Peso had at the moment in one of the stash spots.

"I know where this is comin' from," Donnie said. "How'd you get it?"

"It doesn't matter how I got it. I'm paying you to run it," TT remarked.

"I ain't goin' against Peso. You're gonna have to get somebody else."

Donnie had suspected for a long time that TT was supplying Chato and Paulie with Percocets since Oscar had been the main source on the south side. Peso had passed the word around that anybody selling Percocets to them was going to answer to him. On the sly, Chato and Paulie took small amounts of weed from one of Peso's stash spots to give to TT in exchange for Percocets.

The old woman became angry. "Donnie, I'm asking you to do this for me and you're accusing me of shit. You know what? Fuck you, Donnie! I thought we were better than that."

"A'ight, calm down, TT, damn. I'll find someone else to take it to Minnesota for you, and I'll keep our conversation to myself," he promised. "You're safe. I won't tell Peso on you. What you do over here is your business, not mine."

"I appreciate your offer, Donnie, but I need you to take it. I'll even give you seven grand."

Donnie weighed on it. "I'll do it for you, TT. Just give me until tomorrow."

He did not like the idea of keeping what was going on from Peso. It felt like he was going behind Peso's back, and that wasn't his style. But he also didn't want to get caught in the middle of any problems. As far as Donnie was concerned, he was just a paid runner.

The Next Day—

Donnie prepped the load at TT's place. He decided to make the delivery that evening. Once the stash was secured in the hidden compartment beneath the floorboard, Donnie hit the road. He drove through side streets en route to the nearest expressway.

As Donnie approached the expressway, he clicked on his turn signal and shifted into the turning lane. Before he could make the turn onto the expressway, the red lights of a police car flashed in his rearview mirror, making his heart jump. The police pulled him over.

Just stay cool. Just stay calm, Donnie was introspectively telling himself. *You don't know nothin'. They're stupid. They won't find it. They can't find it.*

The police ordered him out of the car and made him lean against the hood, both hands forward.

"Do you know what I'm stopping you for?" the officer asked.

"Do I look like a mind reader? Sir, I'ont know," Donnie remarked.

The officer smirked. "Well, I pulled you over because you are under suspicion of transporting marijuana."

It was obvious to Donnie that the cops evidently knew in advance he was coming. They radioed in more officers. After half an hour of wondering how in the hell Twelve had found him out, a few more police cars pulled on to the scene. There was a plain-clothes DEA agent who approached, and the scene was crawling with police.

"I want to inspect your vehicle," the DEA agent told him.

"I know my rights, and you can't illegally search my shit," Donnie fired back.

"Well, good thing I have probable cause. Oh, yeah, and this warrant." The agent flashed him the search warrant papers.

Donnie had been sure the stash spot was so well-hidden that the stupid-ass cops wouldn't find it. But his heart sank once the agent seemed to go directly to the floorboard's compartment and discovered the pounds of weed.

"Lock him up!" the agent shouted. Donnie was arrested and placed into the back seat of the agent's car. On the way to the county jail, the DEA agent, driving casually, began questioning Donnie.

"I need to talk to you about something," the agent said in a relaxed tone. "I just want you to know that tomorrow, by dinner, you could be walking out of jail a free man."

"How's that?" Donnie inquired.

"You know Lupe Martinez, aka Peso, don't you?"

"I've heard of him, but I'ont know him."

"Yeah, you know him. That's some of his stuff, isn't it?" the agent said, alluding to the marijuana they found after discovering the stash spot in Donnie's vehicle. "You've got to understand something. We're trying to end this drug trafficking shit—especially through little towns like Racine and Kenosha. I want you to help us."

"I can't help you with that, man," Donnie replied. "That car ain't even mine."

"Bullshit, you were driving it. What do you know about Lupe Martinez?"

"Nothin'."

"Listen, you give me five names and the locations of a couple of stash houses, and I swear you'll be a free man by tomorrow."

Donnie thought about it. Those five people the DEA wanted to know about were homeboys of his. Even if he were to be released the next day, it would look suspicious to a community of people prone to paranoia. He would have to live with the constant fear of someone suspecting that he had snitched, along with what the terror of what those suspicions might lead to. Besides, Peso was a close homeboy. He might be a gangsta, but he had always treated Donnie with the utmost respect.

"Fuck that. I can't help you," Donnie repeated.

Donnie was taken to the Milwaukee County Jail and housed in a federal pod. While sitting in his cell, he pieced together what had happened and came to a chilling realization. He understood who fingered him to the DEA. Donnie had not fallen for the trick, but he was convinced that TT had set him up to take the load. The authorities knew exactly what kind of vehicle to look for, and they had gone directly to the stash.

Donnie was furious. He hadn't fallen for the agent's tricks, but he was certain TT had betrayed him. He wanted TT taken care of.

Chapter 8

Donnie was arraigned before a federal judge in the third-floor courtroom of the federal building. Toya sat quietly in the back. She never really forgave him for abusing her. But after Donnie was arrested, she promised she would be there for him.

Now, Toya had to fend for herself and their nine-year-old son. Most of the cash Donnie had stashed away had been spent on retaining a lawyer for him. Toya had little money left, except what she made from her own hustling. During a visit, Donnie had told Toya that if she needed help, Peso would look out for her.

Several days after Donnie's arraignment, Toya received an unexpected phone call from Peso.

"Hope you a'ight," Peso said. "It's fucked up how Donnie had gotten knocked."

"Thanks for your concern," Toya replied.

"Donnie is a close homeboy of mine and he's always been loyal, so I just wanna show my love and support."

"He told me that I can count on you if I need some help."

"He was right," Peso assured. "If you can come over and see me, I have some things to talk to you about. I wanna help you."

Peso had used her in minor jobs before; picking up money at his dope spots and transporting it to various locations, or renting cars for Raul. She was also an occasional middleman in drug deals for Peso. Though she had spoken to him several times, mostly when Peso needed to get in touch with Donnie, the two had never been formally introduced.

Peso proposed they talk in Lu's, where they would be more comfortable. He had made it a habit of clearing out restaurants and bars before arriving. It was for his own security and the safety of the patrons in case of another ambush.

An hour after their phone conversation, Toya drove over to meet Peso. It was four in the afternoon when she arrived at Lu's Restaurant on National Street. Once she entered the restaurant, she took a seat at a booth, letting one of the men know that she was there to see Peso. Shortly thereafter, Toya saw Peso with two tough-looking men behind him carrying assault rifles.

Before long, she spotted Peso walking toward her, flanked by two tough-looking men carrying assault rifles. By the time she arrived, Lu's had already been cleared out—empty except for the bartender. Peso's shooters had signaled for everyone to leave, ensuring the place was secure. A couple of guards stood posted out front while another watched the back door.

Peso sat down in the dimly lit booth across from Toya. A bottle of Tequila Platinum, his favorite, sat on the table in front of him.

"Once again, I 'pologize for Donnie's arrest. If it hadn't been for TT, Donnie would still be a free man. If I had known beforehand what TT was up to I woulda been able to prevent it," Peso said.

"She is wrong for what she has done, and it needs to be made right somehow," Toya insisted.

"You don't worry about it. I will take care of it. When are you goin' to visit Donnie?"

"Maybe a week from now."

"When you see him, tell him I'll take care of it and not to worry. That's all you need to tell him."

Toya wondered if Peso would kill TT. "What are you going to do to her?" she asked.

Peso took a swig from his glass of tequila. "I'ma run her out of Milwaukee, and I'ma see to it that she has to make a livin' on her own. She won't ever get any help from my family, never," he told her.

"Good. Because she don't deserve any help."

"Speakin' of help, I wanna help you pay bills while Donne is in jail."

Toya eyed him through slits and replied, "I appreciate what you're offering to do for me, but I want you to realize that I don't want any help. I want to do business with you. That money would help pay my bills."

Toya was a hustler, and her business had growing quietly. While Donnie was muling loads for Peso, she had been running her own small drug ring. She would buy a pound or two of weed at a time—often from Peso himself—and distribute it. Few people suspected the cheerful, well-dressed young woman of being a trafficker.

As Toya discussed her experience, Peso realized she was far more involved in the game than he had ever understood. Through Donnie, Peso had occasionally relied on her services, but Donnie had never shared much about her side hustle. Toya was far more ambitious than Donnie had ever been. While Donnie had been content to mule loads and collect his fee, Toya had established her own clientele and was supplying cocaine and marijuana independently.

Peso leaned back in his seat, studying her. "I can see doin' business with you. But I wanna start you off runnin' loads, like Donnie did. I wanna see how you handle it, and then we can talk about frontin' you product," he said.

"Fine with me," Toya replied confidently.

"Here's how things work: I'll pay you five Gs for every load you run. When you're ready to buy, I'll charge twelve hundred a pound. And you'll need to pay a percentage of the hustle fee if you wanna move product in my territory."

Toya's brows furrowed. "What's the hustle fee?"

"It's a fee I use to pay off the Drug Task Force for the right to run the south side," Peso explained. "Anybody under me is protected too—provided they stay in good standing and pay their share of the hustle fee."

"Fair enough. Sounds like you and I are about to make a lot of money together," Toya said with a smirk.

"Let's drink to that," Peso said, raising his glass.

They drank and snorted a couple of lines of coke that Peso's younger cousin had laid out. As the night went on, Peso told her stories about the good times he and Donnie had shared. Toya was impressed. From what Donnie had already told her about Peso, she was beginning to believe in the kingpin's legendary invincibility.

***

Donnie entered the visitation booth, where Toya was waiting on the monitor. Keeping a straight face, he took a seat before the screen and picked up its phone receiver.

"Donnie," Toya began, her tone reserved. "It's good to see you."

"It's good to see you, too, Toya. How are you?" Donnie asked, his voice relaxed but tinged with concern.

"Well, I'm doing what I can to take care of me and your son," Toya replied.

"Already told you, if you need some help, then go to Peso."

Toya leaned back in her seat. "Actually, that's what I'm here to talk with you about. Instead of just getting Peso's help, I'm going to work for him. He wants to pay me to be a runner until I show him that I can handle it."

"Are you sure that's what you wanna do, Toya? Bein' a runner can be way risky in between guys tryin' to rob you and cops out to bust you. Just look at me," Donnie said, gesturing toward his prison surroundings.

"Donnie, you know that I can handle myself. And I'm willing to take the risk."

"But what about our son?"

"I'm doing this to take care of him."

Donnie sighed, realizing her mind was made up. There was nothing he could say to convince her otherwise. "Okay. But make sure you set up your own stash spots. The day you let someone else stash for you is the day you're gonna get caught up," he cautioned. Donnie had taught her how to properly prepare and load a stash spot.

"I will," Toya assured him. "Oh, Peso wanted me to tell you he apologizes for you being in here."

"Well, he doesn't need to feel guilty for what TT did. That old bitch is the reason I'm locked up."

"He also said to tell you not to worry—he'll take care of it."

"You tell him that I 'preciate it," Donnie replied. "Listen, Toya, I'ma be in prison for a while so I won't be there for you and our son. Just make sure you be careful dealin' with Peso."

"I understand. But Peso need to be careful dealing with me too, because I'm not the type of bitch he's used to."

"I know," Donnie chuckled. "Toya, I get that things wasn't always perfect between us. Just know that I love you still."

"I still love you, too."

Toya had fallen in love with Donnie not long after getting out of high school, attracted by his unpredictable lifestyle and humor. However, due to all of his cheating and abuse, she stayed mostly for the sake of their son. Now, with Donnie locked up, she was left to take care of their son alone—and she could handle it.

***

"Lupe, I had no other choice!" TT cried out, staring down the barrel of Peso's Glock.

Peso scoffed. "Choosin' to snitch on Donnie was the wrong choice to make."

Kneeling on the floor, TT begged for her life. " Por favor, Peso. Don't kill me!"

The DEA had approached TT with a proposition similar to the one they made Donnie, promising to use their influence to get her husband, Oscar, out of jail early. She had taken the deal. That was why she had been selling pills. TT was trading Percocets to Peso's boys in exchange for weed, then packaging and smuggling the loads herself. Donnie suspected she'd been the one to tip off the DEA about his run, which was why the narcs had been waiting for him.

After learning that TT was the one who snitched on Donnie, Peso could not allow her to get away with it. He gave TT a surprise visit at her home in order to resolve the problem, holding the older woman at gunpoint.

"I was just doing what I can to try to help Oscar. The DEA promised they would help me if I helped them."

"And if you turned over Donnie, then you'd turn over me," Peso accused, his voice rising with anger.

"I wouldn't do that to you, Lupe. You're like a nephew to me," TT pleaded desperately.

Peso narrowed his eyes, his tone lethal. "TT, you shouldn't have done it at all." He pressed the barrel to her forehead. "I want you to get the fuck outta town. And don't ever come back, or I'll kill you." Peso turned and left out.

For TT, her actions had been an act of devotion to her husband. For Peso, it was an unforgivable act of treachery. If she had not been the wife of his father's close friend—a man Peso considered an uncle—he would have made her pay for it with her life. Instead, he banished her from Milwaukee, ensuring she could no longer benefit from his family's protection.

Chapter 9

During the first month after Donnie's arrest, Toya was all business. She ran about three loads a week for Peso, sometimes going without sleep for two or three days straight. Afterward, she would crash at her apartment, sleeping for nearly twenty-four hours before gearing up for another run. A seventeen-year-old high school dropout—the girlfriend of one of her runners—lived at the apartment and took care of her young son while Toya was gone or catching up on sleep.

Over time, and with Peso's encouragement, Toya built a small operation under the umbrella of his larger one. At first, she only had one helper, someone who had previously run marijuana with Donnie. Toya paid him to drive loads across the border and hand them off to her once they were in safe territory. Her theory was simple: it was worth sacrificing a percentage of her profits to have someone else take the biggest risks. She still ran loads herself within the states, benefiting from Peso's guidance and protection setup.

Peso was impressed with Toya's cool efficiency and nerve. She followed his instructions to the letter. He liked that she was tough and brassy with customers who thought they could withhold money from a bitch. He even liked that she was tough and brassy with him. After she built up some capital, he started selling loads to her outright, giving her the freedom to supply her own clientele.

Toya was shopping at First Lady Boutique, a small but upscale store, being helped by Mona. The two women were familiar with each other because of their shared ties to Peso. Toya wasn't just there for shopping, though. She was waiting to meet up with Peso, but while she waited, she decided to go on a miniature shopping spree, spending a few Gs on clothes and accessories.

While Toya browsed, Mona told her that Peso had called to say he was ready to meet. Stepping out of the boutique, Toya met up with her machine-gun-toting escort, Raymundo. Raymundo was one of her runners, doubling as a bodyguard whenever they were out in the streets. Like Peso's henchmen and steppers, Toya herself carried an assault rifle or a semiautomatic pistol openly and with confidence.

Approaching Peso, who stood in front of Lu's with Paulie, Toya greeted him, "Thanks for making time for me."

"No problema. So, what's up?" Peso replied.

"Well, I got a guy looking to buy twenty-five pounds of smoke and he needs it soon, but I'm all out. So, I was hoping you could front me the product."

"Toya, I'ont have any on hand right now. I'm waitin' for a big shipment to come in," he told her. "Maybe you could convince your buyer to wait until it arrives."

Before she could respond, Peso's iPhone rang, so he stepped away to answer it.

Toya needed the product fast. She had to figure out another way. She turned to Paulie.

"Paulie, do you know anybody with twenty-five pounds?"

"Lemme make a call," he told her, pulling out his iPhone to call Raul.

Before long, Raul showed up in his Range Rover. Toya already knew Raul from the half-dozen times she had seen him around and had helped him take care of business for Peso. Toya began bumping into Raul practically everywhere she went on the south side. If she drove to Peso's stash house to pick up a load, there was Raul lounging around in the house; if she went to Paulie's garage to have her vehicles fitted with a stash spot, there was Raul leaning against the wall. If Peso visited her at her apartment, Raul frequently strode in right behind him, machine-gun in hand. And he became accustomed to seeing her around.

"Paulie said you wanna talk with me," Raul began once Toya climbed into the passenger seat of his whip.

"That's right, I want to talk with you about some business. There's this guy I have who's in need of twenty-five pounds of weed and I need you to front it to me. I asked Peso already and he told me that he doesn't have any right now. So maybe you and I can do some business instead," Toya proposed. She noticed how he stared at her between half-closed eyes as if he seemed bored when she talked, and she didn't know what to make of it. "Are you even listening?" Toya asked, annoyed by his lack of reaction.

Raul shifted towards her, and replied, "Trust I look, listen, and learn. A'ight, I'll front you the pounds. Bring me back twenty-five Gs after you take care of your business." He sold it to her for less than Peso would have charged.

"Sounds good. Just meet up with me at Paulie's auto body shop with the pounds."

"Done," Raul agreed to it.

Paulie's garage specialized in modifying vehicles with hidden compartments designed to transport small amounts of drugs like heroin, cocaine, and marijuana. Although Paulie occasionally did legitimate bodywork, the shop's real business was outfitting smugglers.

At the garage, Raul delivered the product as promised. Toya, mindful of Donnie's advice, declined Paulie's offer to help her load the stash spots. She had learned how to do it herself and was just as good as Donnie had been—maybe even better. Toya carefully packed the pounds of weed into the hidden compartments beneath the floorboards of her vehicle, preparing for another successful run.

***

The next day, Toya texted Raul to meet with her in order to pay him the twenty-five bands for the pounds of weed he had fronted her. Raul suggested that they meet up at McDonald's. Toya drove to Greenfield and Cesar Chavez Street in her Volkswagen Passat. She pulled into the parking lot of McDonald's and parked her whip beside Raul's Range Rover. He stepped out of his whip, then swaggered around to the passenger side of hers, and slid in.

Toya noticed Raul's eyes glance down at the Glock .9 lying in her lap. He found it sexy that she carried herself like a bad bitch. Toya, on the other hand, couldn't deny that Raul's street edge made him attractive. Every time they crossed paths, there was always a lingering exchange of eye contact, but nothing had ever gone beyond business between them.

"Here's your money," Toya said as she pulled out a bankroll from her Birkin handbag, then handed the money to him. "Thanks for helping me out."

Raul pocketed the cash without counting it, and replied, "No problema." He shifted towards her. "I was thinkin' we should work deals together. I have sources of gas and boy, and I have customers of my own but not a good smugglin' operation. But you do."

"And why should I do that?" Toya asked, her tone sharp, cutting straight to business.

"'Cause not only will it help both of our operations, but I'll also sell you product at a better price. I just need your runners to move my loads. I have two-hundred pounds of smoke in wait, and I'll give you fifty once the job's done. All you have to do is send the entire load to a buyer named Rock in Flint, then we'll drive together to Michigan to collect."

Toya's eyes narrowed suspiciously as she leaned back in her seat. "How do I know that I can trust you?"

Raul chuckled. "'Cause you trust Peso, and I'm his right-hand man. If Donnie was out, then I'd have him run the load. Believe me, it's not like I can't find someone else to do it."

"But no one who can get the job done like me. Someone else just might run off or get themselves busted with the load. And we both know you don't care to lose out on that kind of money," she rebutted.

Raul smirked, nodding. "Agreed. So, are you in, or what?"

Toya briefly weighed the offer. The deal was sweet; all she had to do was have someone run the load and she'd be paid with fifty pounds of product. "Okay, I'm in. But out of respect, I wanna talk with Peso about it."

"Then I'll leave that to you. Peso's a man of business, so he'll understand," Raul assured. "Just get in touch with me once you're ready to do the job." He pushed open the door, stepped out of the Volkswagen, and returned to his Range.

The two went their separate ways. Raul knew that having Toya as an asset would help his operation grow, so he needed her to collaborate with him. And Toya figured that doing business with Raul would build her weight and bank up much faster; therefore, she wanted Peso's approval beforehand.

***

Later that week, after running a load for Peso, Toya met up with him at Lu's to collect the rest of her pay. While there, she decided to bring up Raul's proposal. It had been a few days since she and Raul agreed to work deals together, and Toya felt the need to let Peso know. She respected him too much not to let him know beforehand, especially considering how good he'd been to Donnie.

Toya entered Lu's with her shooter, Raymundo, trailing close behind. She immediately spotted Peso seated at a table near the back with Paulie. When he noticed her, Peso waved her over. Toya approached the table, then Paulie stood and stepped away to give them privacy. Raymundo positioned himself near the bar, keeping watch.

"Why don't you have a seat," Peso offered, gesturing to the chair across from him.

Toya sat down gracefully.

"Toya, I can't thank you enough for makin' sure this last load got to where it had to go on such short notice."

"No problem. I just did what you pay me to do," Toya coolly replied.

"And that's why I like doin' business with you." Peso pulled out a stack of cash and handed it to her. "There's a l'il extra for goin' outta your way."

"Thanks." Toya stashed the money inside of her Gucci handbag.

"You earned it."

"Peso, I want to talk with you about doing business with Raul. After he fronted me the twenty-five pounds I needed, we discussed working deals together. He proposed to offer me better prices on weed and heroin if I smuggle loads for him, and I think it's in my best interest in order to build myself up," Toya explained. She observed his reaction closely.

Peso took a swig from his glass of tequila. "I'ont have any objections, as long as I get a percentage of the hustle fee," he told her. "Besides, Raul and you are good friends of mine, so I want y'all to do what's best."

"It's just business between he and I, nothing more."

"I wasn't insinuatin' anything else," Peso replied and tossed his hands up in innocence. He smirked knowingly, though he suspected there might be more between her and Raul someday. But he kept it to himself.

Toya leaned back in her seat and crossed her legs. "I just wanted to clear it with you first—out of respect for you and Donnie. And don't worry, we'll make sure you get your cut of the hustle fee."

"I see Donnie taught you the game well. By the way, how's he holdin' up?"

"He's doing better than before. But he knows he'll have to serve some time in federal prison."

"Next time you see him, tell him to hit me up if he ever needs me, and to keep his head up in there."

"I'll be sure to do that." Toya stood. "I have some other business to tend to, I'll be in touch with you."

"Toya," Peso called after her as she turned for the exit, halting her in her tracks. "You be careful in this game."

"I will."

Toya made her way out of Lu's with Raymundo at her side. She was relieved that Peso respected her decision to do business with Raul henceforth. Now, Toya was focused on building herself up, ready to surpass anything Donnie could have ever imagined.

Chapter 10

Raul had Toya meet him at his stash house to collect the two hundred pounds of weed. She arrived with two of her most reliable runners in an SUV fitted with trap compartments capable of holding a substantial amount of weight. This was the largest load Toya had ever smuggled, and she was determined to ensure it reached its destination without a hitch.

While the runners worked on loading the SUV in the garage, Raul and Toya finalized the remaining details of their business plan. They stood to the side, watching as the pounds were stashed in the faux gas tank and other hidden compartments. Once the SUV was fully packed, Toya gave the green light to her runners to hit the road and deliver the load to Rock, a buyer based in Detroit, Michigan. She and Raul planned to drive out the next day to collect the cash.

Raul led Toya inside the house after the runners had departed. They settled onto the couch in the living room. Raul casually rolled a Backwood filled with grade-A weed as he and Toya continued their conversation.

"Peso told me that he and you talked," Raul said, sparking the blunt and taking a long pull. "That's right," Toya confirmed. "He didn't have any objections with you and I working deals together. Peso just expects for us to pay him our part of the hustle fee."

"He won't have to worry about that. Once we get back from Detroit, we'll give Peso payment for the hustle fee. This is a large shipment that's gonna bring us in plenty of paper. There's a lot on the line."

"Which is why I put my two best runners in charge of this load. But how do you know if you can trust your Detroit clientele with so much money and weed in the mix?" Toya asked.

Raul puffed the blunt. "I'ont know. I never dealt with this nigga before, so I'm sendin' along a couple of shooters in a separate vehicle as security, just in case anything goes down. One thing about this game, you never know the next person's motives. An ally today could be your enemy tomorrow.

"Well, Raul, you don't have to worry about that type of shit with me. As long as you do good by me, then I'll do good by you."

"Same. I have a feelin' that me and you will do good together. There's somethin' about you that I like, Toya," he admitted.

Toya felt herself blush, though she quickly masked it. "And what's that?"

"The way you carry yourself. You don't take shit from nobody and your looks are deceivin'. Most niggas are intimidated by a bitch like you, but not me. I like a down bitch," Raul told her.

"That's sweet of you. And I like you, too, Raul. "But let's try to keep things strictly business between us."

Raul grinned. "If that's what you want, boo."

***

The Next Morning—

After getting a call from Rock the following morning, confirming that he had received the shipment, Raul and Toya made the road trip to Detroit. They brought along a carload of shooters, just in case Rock tried to pull off a jack move. The meet-up was set for a strip mall parking lot, a public spot chosen for its strategic visibility. Toya drove the rented Audi

Q60, circling the lot twice while she and Raul scanned the scene for anything suspicious. Across the street, their shooters waited in an idling car, ready to spring into action if needed. They were certain Rock had his own crew posted up somewhere nearby.

Once they parked in front of a local shoe store, as instructed, Rock emerged from inside. He matched the description Raul had given: a brown-skinned, chubby nigga with six short, blond-tipped wick dreads and tattoos covering his arms and neck. He wore a pair of Cartier Buffalo frames, iced-out jewelry that gleamed under the sun, and Off-White jeans with the stick of a Glock poking out from his waistband. In his hand, he carried a heavy-looking tote bag.

Raul stepped out of the Audi, his Kel-Tec strapped to him by a shoulder harness, swinging casually as he moved. Before shutting the door, he told Toya to keep the engine running in case they needed to make a fast break.

"S'up, my boy. Welcome to the D," Rock greeted.

"Maybe next time I'm here for somethin' other than business you can show me around," Raul suggested.

"I got'chu." Rock held out the tote bag, and said, "Here's your paper. Not a penny short."

Raul collected the bag and gave it a glance. "I'm sure with that load you'll have the best smoke in the D."

"I'll get at you for another one."

"Say less," Raul replied, gripping the bag firmly.

With that, the deal was sealed. Toya watched from the driver's seat as Raul strolled back to the Audi, the bag in hand. The tension in the air lifted slightly, but Toya knew better than to relax completely. In this game, anything could happen—and she wasn't about to let her guard down just yet.

After collecting the money from Rock, Raul and Toya booked a suite at the Hilton Hotel downtown. They planned to make the drive back home first thing in the morning, but tonight they stayed up counting the cash to ensure it was all there. Anticipating a long night, they ordered room service: steaks and a bottle of Rémy Martin VSOP on ice.

Raul dumped all of the stacks of cash from the tote bag onto the comforter of the king-sized bed. He and Toya split the stacks between them and began counting the bills by hand. By the time they were done, the early morning hours had crept in, and the money had come out to the right amount. Raul and Toya lay exhausted on either side of the bed while the money was neatly stacked in between them.

"Who would have thought counting this much money could be so damn exhausting," Toya remarked, lying on her side, propping her head up with one hand. She wasn't accustomed to handling that much money at once.

"Now at least we know that it's all there," Raul replied. For him, counting large sums of cash was just routine. He grabbed the bottle of Rémy, took a swig straight from the bottle, and added, "As long as you keep fuckin' with me, then you'll see more money than you ever even imagined."

Toya grinned and shifted slightly, facing him. "I like how you handle business. I gotta admit, it's kind of attractive."

"What about Donnie?" Raul asked, raising an eyebrow.

"Don't get me wrong—he was good at what he did, but you seem to want more out of this game," she said, her voice soft but firm.

"I can say the same about you," Raul replied, smirking. "Donnie's hustle don't have shit on yours. He's a good guy and all, but I'ont know what you seen in him."

"Donnie took good care of me. He just didn't know how to treat me good."

"Well, if you were mine, I'd treat you better." Raul sat up on edge of the bed. "I'm finna go and hop in the shower real quick."

Toya smiled mischievously. "How about you just take a money shower?" she teased, grabbing a handful of the neatly stacked cash and tossing it into the air. The bills rained down over both of them, some landing on the bed while others scattered across the floor.

Raul laughed, shaking his head, but before he could get up, Toya crawled across the bed toward him and pressed her lips against his. The kiss quickly deepened, and Raul rolled her onto her back atop the bed, the scattered money creating a luxurious, chaotic backdrop. He planted a trail of kisses from her lips down to her collarbone as they began peeling off each other's clothes, tossing them to the floor.

Once they were both naked, Toya pushed Raul onto his back and began sucking his dick. "Shit, girl, you doin' your thang," Raul groaned, watching as she licked her pierced tongue up and down his shaft. The shit felt so damn good to him. She worked her mouth on his dick as if she would be rewarded for her performance, her petite hands stroking his dick while slobbering all over his sac. Toya wanted to make his toes curl. "That's right, eat it off the bone," he uttered, his voice low and raspy. She moaned softly as she gazed into his eyes, her mouth wet and warm. Raul gripped the back of her head, guiding her mouth up and down on his dick while she stared deeply, seductively, into his eyes. Raul could feel his body getting tensed. "You 'bout to make me bust, girl!" Moments later, he released his semen, and Toya allowed it to squirt on her breasts.

"Now fuck me," Toya commanded, climbing onto his lap, straddling him. She clawed his chest as the dick slid deep into her wet, warm pussy. He gripped her small waist firmly, pounding her up and down, loud moans of pleasure and the wet sounds of their passion echoing throughout the room. "Dammit, Raul, I love it so much!" she moaned, riding his dick, rotating her hips and grinding on him with expert precision, her pussy gripping Raul's meat tightly.

Without warning, Raul flipped Toya onto her back in bed, pushing her legs back, and slid his hardness deep inside of her wet-box. He beat the pussy up, causing her to moan his name aloud. While stabbing his dick back and forth in her pussy, Raul leaned down and kissed Toya passionately, their tongues intertwining in a passionate dance. Hooking one of her legs into the crook of his arm, he thrust into her harder, stroking her pussy like one possessed, his sweat mixing with hers as their flesh collided, the bed creaking beneath them. Toya scratched his back with her French-tipped manicure as his dick hit her G-spot repeatedly.

"Yaaassss, baby . . . Make me cummmm!" Toya cooed, her voice breathless. Raul kissed his way down in between her legs, then he used his fingers to spread her swollen, pink pussy lips and flicked his long, warm tongue rapidly over her clitoris. Toya closed her eyes tightly and grabbed a fistful of the bedsheets as her back arched off the bed from the pleasure of Raul's oral sex. "Oooohhhh!" Her body quivered as a wave of orgasm took its course, and Raul tasted her sweet nectar.

Afterward, the two lay on their backs in the bed, still covered with scattered cash. Raul reached over Toya and grabbed the bottle of Rémy from the nightstand, then he took a drink of the liquor before pouring some into Toya's mouth. She giggled softly as the liquid spilled over her lips.

"Toya," Raul began, his tone relaxed as he leaned back against the headboard. "I know you wanted to try to keep shit strictly business between us, but us fuckin' don't change shit. I trust you, and we make a good team, so I want us to take over the game together."

"I'm down," Toya replied. She knew that teaming up with Raul would help her operation grow. And she couldn't deny her growing attraction to him. Raul smirked, taking another swig from the bottle. "Bonnie and Clyde don't have shit on us."

***

During the road trip back to Milwaukee, Raul and Toya opened up to each other, sharing personal stories from their lives. Toya discovered that Raul wasn't just some murderous drug dealer; he told her personal things about his past that revealed a more human side to him. In turn, Raul learned Toya wasn't just a pretty face with a feisty attitude—she shared much about her upbringing, showing depth and resilience. Between these exchanges, the two began to build trust.

To celebrate their first successful deal, Raul and Toya decided to throw a party at Raul's stash house. Only those closely acquainted with them were invited. Paulie and Felix were among the attendees. It wasn't long before Peso showed up with Chato. The atmosphere was lively. Music blasted, tequila flowed freely, and an endless supply of Backwoods filled with grade-A weed kept the vibe going strong.

Toya was one of the only few women among a dozen men. Seated confidently in Raul's lap, she shouted orders in hybrid Spanish, causing playful laughter as the men teased her for her amusing linguistic errors. They started calling her *La Jefa—The Boss*. The name stuck, reflecting the respect she commanded despite the lighthearted teasing.

Peso took a seat on the couch beside Raul, nodding in approval of the festivities. "Glad you made it back safely from your trip to the D, Hermano," Peso said, pouring himself a glass of tequila.

"You and me both," Raul replied. "And all of the money came back right. "Matter of fact, there's me and Toya's part of the hustle fee." He gestured towards the stack of money that sat next to his Glock on the coffee table.

"Good. This will help keep the DTF off all of our backs," Peso said, pocketing the money. Though he hadn't lifted a finger during the Detroit deal—it was Raul's product, and Toya had handled the smuggling and collection—Peso still took his cut for running the territory. In his world, where he was in charge of shit, paying him the hustle fee was a non-negotiable cost of doing business, a privilege to hustle without interference from the Drug Task Force. Raul leaned back and took a drag from a blunt. "Peso, I have a few moves in mind that'll put us on another level. And I want Toya in on it. I'm still workin' out the details as of now, but I'll talk with you once I put shit together," Raul told him.

"I'll be lookin' forward to us havin' that talk," Peso said, taking a sip of his drink. "And I'ont have a problem with Toya bein' in on it. Shorty has proven to be a real asset." Turning his attention to Toya, he added, "Matter fact, I have a move that I will need your assistance with. So be expectin' a call from me soon."

"I'm down to do anything that I can do to help make all of us some money, Peso," Toya assured him.

"Good to know. Just remember that your loyalty is worth more to me than any amount of money," he said, his tone more serious now. Peso wanted Toya to understand that her commitment and reliability were just as important as her abilities. He needed her loyalty, the way Donnie had been.

It didn't go unnoticed that Raul and Toya seemed to be obviously more than just business partners. Peso didn't have anything to say about it. He loved Donnie like a brother; Raul was his friend; he respected Toya. What was going on between them was none of his business. His only priority was ensuring that the operation ran smoothly and that everyone played their part.

Chapter 11

It was nearing winter, and Milwaukee's chilly air made everything feel sharper and colder. A few weeks back, Raul had fronted about ten pounds of weed to a nigga in his mid-twenties named Larry, with the condition that the money would be due on a specific day. That day had come. Raul and Toya pulled up in Raul's Range Rover in front of a shabby, beige-colored duplex on 25th and Greenfield Street. A shiny new Audi truck was parked out front, standing like a sore thumb in the run-down neighborhood.

Raul leaned on the horn, honking repeatedly. The noise brought out a young woman in a dingy pink housecoat, cradling a baby in her arms. Raul stepped out of the Range, followed by Toya, who stood near the whip, observing the situation with caution. Raul approached the woman with his usual no-nonsense demeanor.

"Where's Larry? Is he inside?" Raul asked.

The woman hesitated. "Um, no. He's out of town," she lied, clearly nervous and unsure why Raul was there demanding to see her baby's daddy.

Without warning, Raul brushed past her, barging into the house as if he owned it. He moved with the kind of authority that didn't allow room for objections. Toya stayed outside, leaning against the Range Rover, but she could feel the tension thick in the air.

Inside the house, Raul searched until he found Larry sitting on the edge of a dirty mattress in one of the bedrooms.

Larry was shirtless, wearing jeans and a pair of Air Jordans. His face went pale as Raul entered the room, a mix of fear and resignation washing over him. He knew Raul's reputation. Everybody did. This was a man you didn't cross unless you had a death wish.

"Get up," Raul ordered coldly, motioning for Larry to come outside.

The two men stepped out into the chilly air. Larry, now shivering from both the cold and terror, tried to steady himself. Toya watched from a distance, standing near the vehicle. She could overhear bits of Raul's sharp tone as he laid into Larry.

"Why the fuck do I have to chase your ass down for my fuckin' money, Larry?" Raul demanded, his hands moving animatedly as he spoke, a habit Toya had come to recognize. "Don't make a fool of me. Just give me what you owe."

Toya overheard him telling the young nigga not to make a fool of him, to give him the money he owed.

Larry, visibly shaken, stammered, "I . . . do not have the money right now."

Raul's expression darkened. His voice dropped, calm but laced with danger. "Well, how much money do you have? Just give me that, and we'll call the rest of it quits. Just give me some of the money."

Larry shook his head. "I just told you that I don't have the money. Just give me a few more days and I'll pay you in full. I swear."

Raul's eyes narrowed, flicking toward the shiny new Audi parked outside. "Here it is—you have this brand-new fuckin' whip, but you don't have any paper to pay me at least somethin'. Dawg, you must really think I'm some fuckin' fool-ass nigga!" Raul growled, his voice escalating with every word. Toya, standing a few feet away, knew Raul well enough by now to recognize the signs. He was a man obsessed with respect. Any perceived slight could set him off, and his anger could escalate in a flash. She also knew of his brutal reputation. There were stories—plenty of them—about how Raul had killed more than a few people in fits of rage or on Peso's orders. But even she wasn't prepared for what happened next. Before Larry could respond, Raul's hand moved like lightning to his belt, where his Glock .40 semiautomatic was holstered. He raised the gun, the barrel stopping just inches from Larry's face.

Boom!

The gunshot echoed like thunder in the cold air. The bullet hit Larry dead in between the eyes with the force of a sledgehammer and sent him flying backward into the dirt of the front yard. Toya, frozen in shock, gasped audibly before instinctively jumping back into the Range Rover. She could not believe the swift, irreversible brutality. Her heart pounded as she stared at the scene—Larry's lifeless body sprawled in the dirt, his baby's mother screaming hysterically while clutching the now-fatherless child.

Raul, unfazed, calmly holstered his weapon and walked back to the driver's side of the SUV. He slid into the seat, his expression cold and unreadable as he started the engine. The sound of Larry's baby's mother screaming from the doorway pierced the air, but Raul paid no mind. With a flick of his wrist, he pulled away from the curb, leaving behind the chaos and devastation as if it were just another day.

***

Later that night, at Toya's apartment, the tension lingered in the air. She and Raul sat on the couch, counting money they had collected throughout the day. Toya kept cutting her eyes at Raul, unsure of what to say after witnessing the brutal shooting. Raul noticed her unease.

"Toya, my bad that you had to witness what happened back there. But all the young nigga had to do was give me somethin', anything, so I wouldn't feel like a fool. But the nigga wouldn't do it. He was a scumbag who deserved to die.

He didn't take care of his family. He had come to me with a sob story about bein' broke, that his family was starvin', that his wife needed an operation. I had given him money, then fronted him the weed. I was bein' generous and helpful. Then it turned out the nigga was pushin' a new whip, the one in front of his crib. And he couldn't pay me back. He was makin' a fool out of me, and that was why I smoked his ass," he explained.

Toya did not voice her opinion, but she did not think it was worth killing someone over ten pounds of weed. Raul, however, had often instructed her about his business philosophy.

"It did not matter if someone owed just one dollar or a million," Raul continued. "It should be handled the same way. If you let your guard down, someone is goin' to take advantage of you, or cheat you, and make a fool out of you. I had let my guard down, and see! The nigga tried makin' a fool of me."

While lecturing Toya, Raul prepared a line of cocaine. He snorted the powdery substance through his nostril. Toya observed as he seemed to allow the drug to take its course.

"After we get done countin' this money, how 'bout we go to La Flor de Trigo Bakery," he said, abruptly changing the subject.

Toya took a breath, gathering her thoughts. "Raul, do you ever feel remorse for the murders you committed?" she asked, her voice steady but not probing.

"Nope," he nonchalantly said. "They had to die."

"How do you live with yourself?" Toya pressed. "I mean, how can you live with yourself knowing that you've taken men away from their families, and you've taken young boys out of the life cycle? How do you feel? Don't you ever think about it?"

"Nope."

"Do you ever have bad dreams about it?"

Raul smirked faintly. "No, not really. They had to die."

***

A shipment of heroin that was being sold to a buyer in Minnesota needed Peso's attention, but the drug boss had other priorities. He sent Raul and Toya to drive to the rendezvous to escort the shipment, accompanied by a crew of shooters. They set off in a Chevy Impala, smoking weed as they cruised along I-94 under the cover of night. Traffickers found it prudent to bring drug loads through the highway I-94—it was faster and avoided smaller-town law enforcement scrutiny. But if the authorities attempted to arrest Raul and n'em, then it would come to a gunfight. The authorities would be outnumbered, outgunned, but Toya quickly understood that nobody had planned on any gunplay. It was about getting the job done clean.

The ride went smoothly. No roadblocks. No nosy cops. But the lack of sleep was wearing on them. Raul and Toya had been on the move for nearly 24 hours when they finally reached the rendezvous point right outside of Minnesota to meet up with the buyer, Tito. Once they arrived at the drop destination, they waited to meet up with the buyer at a truck stop. After approximately half an hour, they saw a red SUV pulling into the truck stop. Not far behind was a car full of gunmen. Raul and his men raced up and formed a circle around Tito's vehicles. Everyone got out of the vehicles with the usual show of weapons.

Tito stepped out of the red SUV unnerved. He was one of Peso's most profitable customers. A thin, middle-aged man with gray hair, dark skin and sunken eyes, he had the Twin Cities on lock.

"Where's the cash?" Raul asked, cutting to the chase.

"I have it. But first let me check out the product," Tito requested.

"Cool."

Raul grabbed a brick of *the boy* from the Impala and handed it to Tito. The heroin was wrapped in cellophane. Tito bust open the package and inspected *the boy* carefully, smelling it, feeling it between his fingers, and finally scooping a small amount in his pinky nail and ingesting the brown powdered substance in his nostril. He liked it!

"This is some good product. Here's the money," Tito said as he reached inside his vehicle and collected a backpack that was filled with stacks of money.

"You know that Peso will only send you good quality product," Raul replied as he grabbed the backpack. "And I hope you'll never shortchange him."

"Peso is a good guy so I would never. All the money is there. Tell Peso that I'll be in touch with him as soon as I need to re-up."

With the payment handled, the product became Tito's responsibility. He planned to have one of his men transport the shipment back to his final destination. Standing in the bright headlights of one of the vehicles, Raul and Tito jabbered away like old friends as one of Tito's vehicles was being loaded with the product by his men.

Raul pointed in the direction of a white SUV that one of his shooters had brought. Toya noticed a quick exchange of nods among the men. Then she saw the shooter slide out of the white SUV. Two of Tito's men jumped in and drove off, with the rest of Tito's men tailing the white SUV. It hit Toya then—Raul had planned for this. He had brought the white vehicle on purpose. The white SUV wasn't just part of the caravan; it was a deliberate decoy. If anyone tried to intercept the shipment, they'd hit the wrong vehicle. Raul's foresight impressed her yet again.

***

By the time Raul and Toya got back to Milwaukee, they had gone without sleep for two days in a non-stop whirl of activity. Exhausted, they crashed in one of Peso's stash houses.

Toya could have slept for half a day, but at about ten o'clock that night, noise from a party in the front room kept waking her up. Chato, Peso's younger cousin, didn't help matters either—he kept coming into the room to get cocaine from a stash she and Raul had on the dresser. Finally, Toya gave up on sleep and headed to the kitchen to heat up leftover pizza.

While the microwave hummed, she glanced into the front room, where Peso was deep in conversation with Captain Danielson, head of the Drug Task Force. Despite his position in law enforcement, Danielson always seemed cozy with the drug dealers. Every time Toya saw him, he was either sipping liquor or smoking a blunt. Though polite, their interactions had always been minimal—Toya didn't trust him, and she suspected the feeling was mutual.

More than a dozen other people who were linked in one way or another to Peso's organization crowded around the front room. Music blared from the stereo. All of the partygoers were armed with assault rifles or semiautomatic pistols. One of the gunmen was holding an AR-15 horizontally at chest level. On the flat of the grooved ammunition clip were white lines, and someone standing in front of the gunman was snorting the lines directly from the clip. It was a snort style considered 'muy macho' by the gun-toting drug dealers.

Toya stayed with the partygoers just long enough to microwave the pizza and went groggily back to the room. She and Raul were awakened the following day at noon by Chato, who needed more cocaine from their stash.

"Peso is about to get up and will be heated if coke isn't prepared for him," Chato explained.

As he gave Chato what he needed, Raul asked, "What was the big deal last night?"

Captain Danielson had come by to pick up the hustle fee from Peso, he told them before leaving the bedroom.

Raul had known in advance about the hustle fee payoff but had completely forgotten. If he had not been stretched to the limits of endurance by the hectic pace of recent days, he would have attended. After tossing on his clothes, Raul grabbed the backpack that he had received from Tito for the shipment and made his way out of the room, leaving Toya in bed. He was on his way to go and see Peso. Once he entered the front room, there was Peso seated on the couch snorting a line of coke. Raul stepped over to the couch and placed the backpack on the coffee table in front of them, then took a seat beside Peso.

"The shipment to Tito got to him without a problem. There's the payment," Raul told him.

Peso unzipped the backpack and saw numerous stacks of blue strips inside. "Good job. Remind me to count the payment later," he replied.

"Will do. Speakin' of payments, I see you took care of Captain Danielson."

"Now we don't have to worry about his task force much at all. That said, I want to put more product in the streets."

"Sounds like a plan to me," Raul agreed. He'd been thinking about expanding their inner city operation beyond just the south side of town, and in due time he would act upon his idea. "And I'm sure Toya is down with it."

Peso leaned back, a thoughtful expression crossing his face. "Raul, Toya is a valuable asset to the both of us. So far, she has brought a lot to the table. Even still, remember that you have to be the one makin' the major decisions if you're goin' to have her in on moves," Peso said firmly. He wanted his underboss to understand that it was on him to call the shots. Peso believed that Raul had the potential to one day be in charge of the entire operation.

Chapter 12

The pace of what Peso set was frenetic, his life now consumed by nonstop activity. He and those under his wing sometimes went for two or three days without sleep, handling the grueling business of drug trafficking: obtaining *boy* and weed, transporting drugs to the border, getting across the border safely, cutting deals with clientele, collecting money, and laundering it. Then there were time-consuming ancillary activities to be attended to, such as arranging for vehicles to be stolen and brought to the south side, smoothing out distribution problems at some trap spots, maintaining a relationship with the DTF and a myriad of other tasks that placed heavy demands on his time.

It had been a few days since Peso mentioned needing Toya's assistance. He finally called her and scheduled a meet.

Peso dropped by Toya's place to discuss the business he needed her to handle immediately. Once she let him inside of her place, they took a seat on the couch in the living room.

"So, what is it you need my help with?" Toya asked, cutting to the chase.

"Since you'll be takin' a trip to drop off a load of mine in Chicago, I need you to arrange a meet with those guys there that you told me about. I have a big job for them," Peso told her.

"Just name the time and place."

"I want you to drive them back to Milwaukee put them up at a motel until I can meet with them."

"Done. And what exactly is it you want with them?"

"You told me that they're good at gettin' cars. Well, I want you to place an order with them to get a car that can carry a big load, and I need it delivered within a week," Peso instructed.

He did not explain why it was needed so soon, but she knew better than to ask. Peso did not use the word "steal" when he spoke to her about the vehicle, but that was the implication. He almost never bought anything—at least, not from its rightful owner. He merely sent someone to take it and then paid the thief, usually in pounds of weed or in grams of *boy*.

"What kind of car do you want?" Toya asked.

"An SUV," Peso said.

"Any particular model?"

"It doesn't matter. As long as it is low-key."

"Alright. Once I drop off your load while in Chicago, then I'll contact them."

"Say no more."

The next day, Toya delivered the load of weed to the customer in Chicago. Afterwards, she contacted Dan and Sleazy and asked them to meet up with her. Soon thereafter, Toya met them beneath the L train tracks. She stepped out of her car and approached Dan and Sleazy.

"So, what's up?" Dan greeted. He knew that the only reason Toya would call them is to do some business.

"I have a big job lined up for you two, if you're up to it," Toya said.

"That depends," Sleazy piped in. "What's the job and how much does it pay?"

"I'm not in a position to negotiate the price," she told them. "You will have to go to Milwaukee and work that out with Peso."

"Wait. You mean to tell us that you work for Peso?" Dan asked. Like many, he had heard all about the drug lord.

"Yes, that's what I'm telling you. And he wants you two to get him an SUV that's inconspicuous that you can transport a major load in for him. Are you in?"

"Yeah, we're in," Dan spoke on both of their behalf.

"And when is this all supposed to go down?" Sleazy inquired.

"How about we go and see Peso? He'll give you all the details," Toya replied. "You two can ride with me. I'll be leaving later tonight after I let Peso know that you're on board."

Once the arrangements were made, Toya called up Peso and informed him that Dan and Sleazy had agreed to meet with him. These guys were her discovery. A dealer she knew had introduced her to them during one of her recent drug runs to Indiana. When the guys learned that Toya worked for Peso, the infamous narco honcho of Milwaukee, they were most definitely interested in smuggling for him.

***

Back in Milwaukee a few hours later, Toya drove the two men downtown and booked them a room at the Hilton Hotel. They were instructed to wait there while Peso handled other pressing business. There was just too much going on in the city during this week, and nobody, particularly Peso, could make any time for them. A load of cocaine that was being shipped in from Miami also needed Peso's attention.

As Dan and Sleazy settled in, Raul stopped by the hotel to check them out and confirm they were legit. Raul was skeptical of doing business with people they didn't know and trust, despite Toya vouching for them. He needed to see for himself.

Raul knocked on the hotel room door, which was opened moments later by Dan, a tall white guy with long hair.

Without speaking, Dan stepped aside, letting Raul in. Inside, Sleazy—a dark-skinned nigga—was lounging on the couch. The pair quickly recognized that Raul wasn't just any crew member. They figured Raul must be the drug lord the way he carried himself. The bust-down Cuban link around his neck, the Rolex on his wrist, and the Glock with an extended clip protruding from his waist signaled his status. They were immediately impressed.

"You must be Peso," Dan said.

Raul shook his head in the negative. "I just dropped by to tell y'all that Peso would probably be able to see y'all tomorrow. There's just too much goin' on at once for him to make time today," he laid out.

"And why couldn't he have had Toya tell us that instead?" Sleazy asked, his tone bordering on disrespect.

"'Cause she's already done her part. Now y'all business is with Peso, and I'm here on his behalf," Raul replied coldly, fixing Sleazy with a hard glare.

"That's cool," Dan quickly interjected, trying to diffuse the tension. "We'll be here whenever Peso has time to discuss things. But while we're waiting, do you have any weed to take off some of the edge?"

"Yeah, I got you. Just give me some time and I'll be back with it ASAP. In the meantime, just be patient and Peso will get to you two once he's able."

Raul left the hotel, satisfied the pair were who they claimed to be, although Sleazy's attitude had rubbed him the wrong way. He planned to share his impressions with Peso. An hour later, Raul returned with an ounce of weed in a Ziploc bag for them to smoke while they waited to meet with the drug lord.

***

The runners ended up waiting an entire day for Peso to become available. Around noon, Raul and Toya stopped by the hotel, picked them up, and drove them to one of Peso's stash houses.

Inside, Peso was sitting on the edge of a couch, a blunt in one hand and a Draco with a drum magazine resting in his lap, its barrel pointing forward. Diamonds gleamed from his neck and wrists, and piles of cash littered the coffee table in front of him. He looked every bit the part of a thugged-out Mexican drug boss who controlled a significant portion of crime in the Midwest.

The stash house was packed with Peso's shooters, each armed to the teeth with AR-15s, Dracos, and Glocks fitted with extended magazines. At a snap of Peso's fingers, they were on their feet, ready to shoot to kill if necessary. The rest of the time, their job was to stand around looking menacing—cold, hostile glares fixed on anyone new who stepped into their space. They didn't need much prompting to carry out their roles; it came naturally.

Dan and Sleazy, despite being experienced road runners, were a bit unnerved by the tension in the room. Constant danger had made them cocky, but this was Peso's world, and it was different from the one they were used to.

Toya had juiced the runners during the trip to Milwaukee to find out prices they had in mind and had passed the information on to Peso. They had been getting twenty bands a load from other traffickers, but they were convinced they could get at least fifty bands per load out of Peso. The runners had a package deal in mind for the amount.

Peso, Dan, and Sleazy took seats on the couches while everyone else stood on alert. The runners had expected Peso to look like a boss, but they were still surprised by the sheer intensity of his aura. Conversely, Peso hadn't expected the runners to be a suburban-looking white guy and a ghetto-styled black dude. Still, as long as the deal worked out, appearances didn't matter.

Dan, doing most of the talking, pitched their years of smuggling experience, peppered with entertaining stories of their exploits. Peso asked plenty of questions, laughed at their anecdotes, and shared some of his own. But when it came time to talk numbers, the smiles disappeared.

Peso hit the blunt, exhaling a cloud of smoke, and said, "So, what's it gonna cost to have you two run major loads from Mexico to Wisconsin?"

"How about fifty thousand per load?" Dan proposed. "All you'd need to do is arrange for a crew in Mexico to load the product, another crew in Wisconsin to offload it, and security to tail us for protection. For an additional fee, we can deliver it straight to the final destination."

"And we want our payment in drugs, not cash," Sleazy clarified.

"Fifty Gs?" Peso said, pretending he had heard the figure for the first time. He shook his head. "I'll give you thirty Gs a load instead."

"Absolutely not. We have the experience that you need. And we can get our own vehicles. Plus, these are major loads, so it's worth our price," Dan insisted.

"I'ont care," Peso responded. "I have people that ain't as experienced, and they do a good job for me. And they don't cost me what you guys want."

"But they won't get the job done as fast as us. We know what we're doing."

Peso leaned back coolly, puffing on the blunt. "Do this job first, then maybe I'll pay you more. I need to see what you can do before I throw fifty bands your way."

Toya, sensing the growing frustration in the runners, leaned forward and said, "If you'll just listen to him and quit interrupting, you'll understand what he's saying."

From experience, Toya knew how Peso operated. When drug buyers came to him for the first time, he usually hiked the price to about twice what he sold to other people. When he was satisfied the newcomers knew what they were doing and had good connections for moving the drugs, he would bring the price down. Toya figured Peso was going to use the same approach with these runners. He would test them out on a couple of loads, and if they really did everything they said they could do, then he would give them fifty racks a load. But not beforehand.

Sleazy remarked, without even looking at Toya, "We don't need no woman discussing our business."

It was the wrong thing to say. Raul's eyes narrowed dangerously.

Peso stood up and said, "I'd listen to her any day before I'd listen to you." He disappeared into the kitchen, and when he came back he had the blunt between his lips. He said, "We'll discuss it some other time. I'll call you."

The runners, tense and bristling, left the stash house, marching through the screen door to their vehicle. Weapons rattled in the background as Peso's shooters kept their eyes locked on them.

On the way back to the hotel, Toya turned in her seat to address the runners. "Y'all need to understand his side. This is a very powerful man in his own territory. He's never seen you before. And honestly, the way you disrespected me in front of him didn't help your case. I'm the one who introduced you to him—you can't do that."

Sleazy scoffed, "Shorty, you made him sound like he owns the whole of Milwaukee. He's just a small-timer. We didn't come here to play kid games."

Raul had not said anything the whole time. Now he leaned forward against the steering wheel, reached behind his back and pulled the Glizzy out of his Gucci belt. He put it on the seat in plain view of the runners and put his hand over it. They could see his fingers tapping on the barrel, near the trigger.

Toya turned around, batted her eyes, and said with an exaggerated sweetness, "We don't play games either."

Nobody said anything for the rest of the commute. Once there, Raul and Toya followed the runners to the entrance. Raul was still holding the blick, and Toya was hoping he would not do something stupid. It looked like they had taken a couple of hostages, but they were just escorting them. When they separated at the entrance of the hotel, the runners had their eyes on Raul's blick.

Toya said cheerfully, "Talk to you later."

Once in their vehicle, Raul exploded. He slammed his fist against the steering wheel. He aimed the gun at the windshield, and Toya thought he really was going to shoot.

"Nobody gets away with talkin' that way!" he yelled.

Toya tried to calm him down. "What are you getting so heated about? They're just cocky sons-a-bitches who think they can get their own way by flaunting their experience. Peso wouldn't give a damn if they were the best. They're going to have to do it his way if they want his business."

Raul finally called Peso's cellphone and told him about the conversation.

Peso said, "We're not gonna play kid games. I'm gonna let them take a load for thirty Gs, but only pay them twenty Gs. Then they're gonna have to work another load for twenty Gs, and I'll give them ten Gs for that. The third load they take, if they're still down to run for me, I'll give them the fifty Gs plus the twenty Gs I owe them."

"When do you want to see them again?" Raul asked.

"Tell them in two or three days. Make them wait."

Later that day, Toya went alone to talk to Dan and Sleazy. They finally agreed to Peso's terms.

Chapter 13

"Find me somebody to run this load," Peso told his younger cousin.

"I'll take care of it," Chato assured.

On the day the load was supposed to leave, all of Peso's experienced runners were already on the road or were not available for one reason or another, including Dan and Sleazy.

Chato went out in search of someone to run the load. He had two guys in mind that had been asking for a chance to prove themselves. Chato came back with two pack boys from around the neighborhood. One had light brown hair and freckles; the other was dark-skinned with coal-black hair and piercing eyes. Like most young hustlers on the south side, they had worked at one time or another for more established players in the game. The freckled-faced one had once driven a load of weed to Madison, Wisconsin, proving to Peso that he at least had the nerve to run product. Both of them were eager—eager to work for the infamous drug boss and even more eager to pocket the money that a few hours of driving would bring them—far more than they could ever make in a month pushing packs in a trap spot.

The Mercedes-Benz Sprinter van was loaded at one of Peso's stash houses on a brisk fall evening. Peso leaned against the van and shouted orders to the two pack boys and several of his workers out in the yard who had been assigned to help load up the van. As usual, Raul, Toya, Chato, and some of Peso's other men were bunched around, standing near Peso.

The two pack boys loaded the marijuana bales into the van's hidden stash compartments as quickly as they could. Every so often, they glanced over at the dealers. They eyed the machine guns hanging around their necks, the Glocks stuffed into their waistbands, and even the weapon carried by Toya. She wasn't just a "pretty face"—she was strapped like the rest of them. The sight inspired both envy and a tinge of fear in the rookie runners. When the loading was finished, Raul gave them some expense money, detailed instructions, and a Ziploc of weed for the road. "Follow the directions I gave you exactly. No shortcuts, no fuck-ups," Raul warned. Soon, they were off to the highway. Two gunmen followed them in another vehicle to make sure they got to the highway without any trouble. By the time they arrived, it would already be dark and safer to road-run. From then on, until the delivery, the rookie weed runners were on their own.

Back at the stash house, Peso was already immersed in other business—arranging drug deals, coordinating shipments, and setting up future plays. The two rookie runners in the Sprinter van were the furthest thing from his mind. He had his money lined up, the weed was en route, and the deal was practically ancient history. But early the next morning Peso got a FaceTime call that turned his mood foul. The marijuana buyer from Iowa appeared on the screen, his face twisted in anger.

"Where are my fuckin' birds?" the buyer demanded, referring to the marijuana. "Did they fly away, or what?"

"Listen, don't get so damn heated," said Peso. "I'll call you back once I figure out what the fuck is goin' on."

"You do that," the buyer snapped before ending the call.

Raul looked confused: "Is everything a'ight, Peso?"

"Hell naw! The load hasn't even gotten to the buyer yet. Y'all find out what happened to those two fuckin' guys with the load," he ordered, pointing at Toya and several other people.

Toya made calls to her connections while others hurried out to pay visits to anybody even remotely related to the pack boys to find out what happened to them. Had they been busted on the highway? If anybody knew, it would be one of the relatives. But nobody had heard a thing—not even a whisper about the runners or the Sprinter van.

Peso was livid, pacing back and forth with a fury that made everyone in the stash house tread lightly. "If they had not been busted, the only other possible explanation was that they had stolen the load. That's what I got for usin' someone I didn't know well," he griped. "If they had ripped me off, I would have to make good on the load by replacin' it."

Raul, standing nearby, nodded grimly. "If they ripped you off, it's not just about the money or the weed. Word will get around that you got jacked by a couple of peons. That's bad for business. It'll make you look weak, like you ain't in control."

Peso's eyes narrowed, his tone cold as steel. "I'm gonna kill those sons of bitches!"

He knew that the runners, like homing pigeons, would sooner or later flutter back to their residence. Then they would have some explaining to do. To Peso, drug boss of Milwaukee, it did not matter if it was thirty pounds, three hundred pounds or three thousand pounds. If they had stolen from him, he would make them pay for it.

***

Several hours after the runners had first left for Iowa, Peso got a call from them.

"Where the hell is the load?" Peso demanded.

"About that . . ." the freckled-face runner began nervously. "We got into an accident out on the highway and abandoned the load. We were smoking the weed Raul had given us and my boy was not paying sufficient attention, and then suddenly, *bang!* We were in a ditch, nearly tipped over."

"That's bullshit!" Peso barked.

"Trust us, we would never bullshit you."

Peso scoffed. "I don't trust many," he muttered darkly. "Where are you two right now?"

"We're at the Motel 8 on the outskirts of town," the freckled-face runner told him.

"Stay put."

Peso hung up and immediately called his top people. Within minutes, he and his crew were on their way to the motel.

The two failed runners sat nervously in their motel room, their eyes glazed and their throats dry. They themselves had called the drug boss as soon as they could, hoping they could explain the accident and avoid the worst. They were not experienced runners, but they knew the risks. The moment they agreed to run the load, their lives had become collateral. It was a code they had absorbed practically with their mother's milk. Running might buy them time, but hiding wasn't an option—not from someone like Peso. Their only hope was to face him, explain what happened, and pray for mercy. They were discussing how to explain it to Peso, expecting the worst to happen, when the door of their motel room burst open. Peso, Raul, Chato, Toya, and several gunmen stormed in, weapons at the ready.

Before they could say a word, Peso and Raul grabbed the young men by their collars, shaking and slapping them.

"What did you do with the product?" Peso growled.

"Where is the van?" Raul demanded.

Peso and Raul kept shouting variations of the same question without giving the young men a chance to even speak. Like a crowd at a boxing match, everyone was shouting. The two trembling pack boys begged for a chance to speak.

Peso's grip on the collar of the freckled-face youngster finally relaxed. He turned to Raul. "That's enough. Let 'em talk, and let's see what they have to say. And 'then' we kill 'em."

Almost in unison, the two runners gasped, "We didn't steal the product. We had an accident!"

"It's like I told you before, we had run into a ditch ten miles after hitting the highway. It was pitch-black out there, the road was winding, and we didn't see the curve until it was too late. The van didn't tip over, but we couldn't get it out of the ditch," Freckled-face explained once again.

"You lyin' motherfuckers. What took you so fuckin' long to call me?" Peso demanded an answer.

"There was no phone service and it took us that long to get back to Milwaukee. We had to walk on the highway," said the second runner, his voice trembling.

Peso's eyes narrowed. "You better be able to take us to that van and that product better be there, 'cause if it's not, you're goin' to die."

The runners were dragged from the motel and shoved into one of several vehicles parked in front of the motel restaurant. Including the pack boys, there were a dozen people in the group. The caravan consisted of three cars and an SUV, all bristling with weaponry. Each vehicle carried heavily armed men armed with AR-15s, Dracos, and semiautomatic pistols. They drove to Peso's stash house to pick up ammunition, then headed west to the highway leading to Iowa.

Peso rode in the lead car with Chato, Felix, and the two runners. As always, he insisted on leading the pack.

They arrived at a truck stop just before midnight and parked their vehicles in a tight formation. The headlights illuminated the parking lot as the gang disembarked, their weapons clattering in the silence. The runners remained in the car, their faces pale.

Felix was having second thoughts about going to check out the van. He strode to the edge of the truck stop. "This idea sucks," he said. "We don't know what's up the road. Those two niggas could have been caught and then worked out a deal to get us to come. Or the truck could really be in a ditch, but it's been found and they're waitin' for someone to come for it."

"You may be right. But we have to at least go and see," Peso replied. He turned to the crew. "Everyone turn off your headlights."

The moon was not out but the sky was bright with stars. They could barely make out the road ahead of them. Peso had brought along a stock of blunts that Chato had rolled up earlier that day. Chato passed out some blunts and everyone lit up, and soon the orange tips of blunts moved around in the darkness like crazy fireflies.

For about ten minutes they debated whether anyone should go to scout the van, then Peso fell into a reflective silence. He knew one day he was going to die a violent death. That was the way it had to be. But was it going to be tonight? Over a bullshit Sprinter van? He formed a mental image of a tiny army of smugglers in machine-gun battle with a platoon of narcs. It appealed to him.

Finally, he spoke. "Fuck it. We all go. If they're out there waitin' for us, we're goin' to take a bunch of 'em with us."

Toya was getting cold feet at the thought of a suicidal showdown with narcs. Peso shared his vision of a shootout if there were any agents out there waiting to bust them. He had always made it clear—nobody with a badge was ever going to take him alive.

"I don't really want to do this," Toya said. "I'll wait over here."

Raul firmly said, "You comin' with us. We all go together."

The gang entered their vehicles and drove towards the destination where the van was supposed to be stuck in a ditch. Peso's gunmen aimed their machine guns out the windows, just in case. If it was setup, it would have to happen in the area of the van somewhere up the road. They knew how the authorities operated. The DEA would wait for them to get to the drug-filled van and unload the product before making a bust that had a chance of standing up in court.

The headlights of their vehicles illuminated the area. Raul, Toya, and their gunmen were already at the junction when Peso's vehicles pulled up. They drove in single file three miles farther before spotting the van. It was leaning at a dangerous angle into an arroyo next to the road, just as the runners had described. Peso sent two of the vehicles to scout around. They came back ten minutes later. The coast was clear.

Everyone approached the Sprinter van with their weapons leading the way. So far, no one had ambushed them. It appeared that the van had not been bothered.

Raul entered the van and loosened one of the floorboards covering the hidden compartment. "It's all here!"

Clearly, the only way to recover the van was to build a makeshift path leading back to the road. The pack boys and gunmen were put to work building a base of rocks so the van could be jacked up higher and higher.

Peso sat on the hood of one of the vehicles, patiently smoking a blunt with Raul and Felix and watched the work, illuminated by the headlamps of one of the vehicles. Nearly an hour later, when the work was finally done, Raul jumped behind the steering wheel and expertly backed the van onto the road.

The pack boys had done most of the hard labor and were as filthy as coal miners by the end of it. They were standing next to the van. They watched Peso slide from the hood of his vehicle and walk toward them holding his Draco. A blunt was dangling from his lips.

"That was stupid of you to drive into a ditch," Peso said, his eyes narrowing and unsmiling.

The faces of the drug runners showed they expected the worst.

"But you did the right thing goin' back to Milwaukee to find me," Peso continued. "My apologies for mistrustin' you two. I trusted people again and again, and how many times have I been ripped off? How much money had I lost by trustin' people I shouldn't have trusted? Too many times!"

Peso broke into a long, convoluted explanation about how he had become mistrustful of people, and how this suspicion had been forged through repeated betrayal. The two runners listened intently, caught between relief and unease. The two runners had been victims of other people's untrustworthiness.

Toya and Raul had exchanged knowing glances—they'd heard the same complaint again and again. Anyone who spent even one evening with Peso, smoking blunts and sipping tequila until the early morning, knew that this complaint was a constant refrain. But unlike the naive runners, Raul and Toya also knew the darker side of Peso's paranoia—what 'really' happened to people who tried to double-cross Peso.

"Do you have any money?" Peso asked.

"No, big homie," one of the runners replied, shaking his head.

Peso pulled out a wad of money from the pocket of his stacked jeans and gave the filthy men $500 each. "Then take this. And be careful not to fuck up by drivin' into any more ditches. Be safe."

"Thanks a lot!" one of the runners stammered, gratitude washing over him like a benediction from a rural priest. Toya thought for an instant that the pack boys would go to their knees and kiss Peso's hands.

They were hicks but not fools. Wasting no time, the runners hopped into the van, slammed it into gear, and sped off westward, careful not to make another mistake that could cost them their lives.

Peso and his entourage stood in the road and watched the van's taillights until they disappeared over a hill. Then everybody piled back into the vehicles and returned leisurely to Milwaukee. During the drive Peso dialed up the buyer.

"Your birds are flyin' to you as we speak," Peso told him.

"Thanks for everything, Peso. I knew that I could count on you," the buyer replied.

Peso hung up and leaned back in his seat. One thing was certain—Peso always delivered. His ability to maintain a reputation for reliability was part of what kept him on top of the game. But he also knew, all too well, that plenty of people were waiting for the chance to take him down.

Chapter 14

A white Mercedes-Benz G-Wagon drove slowly over the parking lot of Mitchel International Airport. The driver, an expert at running loads all across state lines, spotted the Range Rover. Knowing who was inside of it, he parked the truck near the Range in the lot.

Moments later, a Chevrolet Equinox pulled up beside the G-Wagon. Men armed with assault rifles jumped out of the Equinox, standing guard as Peso walked up to the wagon. The driver of the G-Wagon killed the engine, and Peso signaled to his men to get to work. Moving quickly and efficiently, the men unloaded the cargo: a sturdy cardboard box, four feet long, three feet wide, and a foot deep. As the box was tossed into the trunk of the Equinox, Peso opened it to inspect the contents. Inside were kilogram packages, each about the size and shape of a thick hardcover book, tightly wrapped in green, silver, or gray plastic tape. Each package was marked with symbols and numbers written in indelible ink. When the box was loaded onto the Equinox, Peso signaled for the driver to leave.

Once the box was secure, the driver of the G-Wagon left, already speeding onto the expressway. The Range Rover and Equinox followed shortly after, rumbling through Milwaukee's streets toward one of Peso's stash houses. Upon arrival, the box was carried inside. Peso grabbed one of the tightly wrapped bricks, pulled out a knife, and sliced it open. As everyone crowded around, he scooped a couple of ounces of fine white powder into a Ziploc bag and held it up for the crew to see.

"From now on we'll also be movin' cocaine," Peso declared. "With my connect, we'll be receivin' shipments of bricks of white on the regular. So I'll need all of you to pull your weight and find clientele for the product," Peso told his crew.

Raul, standing near the coffee table, voiced his concerns. "Peso, we already have beef with niggas. Now that we're about to start floodin' the streets with more product and make more money, we're goin' to accumulate even more beef."

Chato, ever hot-headed, whipped out his Glock and waved it with a grin. "Then we'll smoke whoever want any beef with us."

"I understand what you sayin', Raul," said Peso. "But we all know that beef is somethin' that comes with the game. It won't stop us from gettin' money."

"Let's not forget that we still have beef with the nigga Junior," Chato reminded. "I ain't lettin' that shit go."

Peso exhaled and gave his younger cousin a reassuring look. "Don't trip, l'il cuz, we gonna deal with him when the time comes," Peso told him. He then tossed the Ziploc bag on the coffee table. "Why don't everyone enjoy a sample of the pure."

While some of the crew indulged in the powder, Peso stepped out of the room. He wanted to phone his connect in private.

"Peso, I assume you received the shipment," Manuel said once he answered the call.

"Yeah, I did," Peso responded.

"Good. Hopefully you won't have a problem moving it."

"Believe me, I can solve my problems. Once I'm done movin' this shipment, then I'll be in touch with you."

"I'll be waiting. If all goes well, then we can talk more about upping the stakes," Manuel suggested.

"Sounds good."

Peso ended the call. He knew that all he had to do was flood the streets in order to get rid of the bricks. It was time to distribute a load of twenty bricks of pure cocaine that had just arrived from his connect in Miami.

***

In between Peso's organization moving loads of marijuana, heroin, and now cocaine, money was rolling in abundantly. With the hustle fee in effect, the Drug Task Force turned a blind eye to all of the drugs being moved by Peso's team. However, there were still some drug busts that were out of Captain Danielson's control. But not enough to put a dent in the drug infestation on the south side.

After a while, Raul and Toya essentially worked for themselves, paying Peso a percentage of the hustle fee for the right to operate in his territory. They also gave Peso a helping hand whenever they were needed. They decided that they wanted to move their base of operations to the north side, but needed to obtain Peso's blessing. Without his approval, they would have a tough time moving their product through the streets without the DTF sweating them.

Raul and Toya entered Lu's. They were there to discuss business with Peso. It was later in the evening, so the place was occupied with patrons. Raul greeted Felix and Chato, who sat at the bar having drinks.

Where's Peso?" Raul asked.

"He's in the back office," Chato said.

"Why don't you sit down and have a drink with us?" Felix said and then downed a shot of tequila.

"Maybe later. I have some business to take care of." Raul looked to Toya. "Stay here and have a drink with the fellas while I talk with Peso."

Once Raul stepped into the office, he found Peso perched on front of the desk talking on his iPhone. As he entered, Peso was wrapping up his call with Manuel about another load. Thus far, business with the Miami connect was going well.

"Peso, here's the money from the product." Raul handed over a tote bag filled with cash.

"I can always count on you to get shit done," Peso said as sat the tote bag beside him on top of the desk.

"Fa sho. And I can get more done if we expand the operations."

Peso looked curious. "What are you tryin' to say?"

"I'm tryin' to say that me and Toya decided that we're goin' to open up shop on the north side. And I'm hopin' that you'll greenlight it."

When Raul told him about their decision, Peso tried to talk him out of it.

"Wait a second, Raul. You don't know the north side well enough," Peso pointed out. "It won't take long for twelve to know who you are. They would end up tailin' you everywhere to look for a way to bring you down, and you cannot get protection like on the south side, so it's best just to stay on the south side and let the runners take all the risks."

Raul scoffed. "Listen, Peso, I understand what you're tellin' me but I know how to handle myself. Besides, Toya is from the north side, so she knows it like the back of her hand, and I'm sure she'll teach me all about that part of town." He was adamant.

"You're doin' just fine on the south side of town. Why do you want to switch things up now, Raul?"

"It's not like we haven't talked about the idea of this before. We both know there's lots more paper for us to make if we expand our operations to the north side also. All I'm askin' for is your approval."

Peso let out a sigh. "A'ight, Raul. I'll back you on this. But the first time somethin' goes wrong, then I advise you to shut down shop." He finally gave up trying to dissuade him.

"Nothin' will go wrong. All I have to do is trust in Toya," Raul told him. "I 'preciate the blessing. Now I'm about to go and have a drink with Toya and the guys."

"Why don't you send Toya to see me for a second?"

"I got you."

Peso sent for Toya and lectured her sternly, like a father. "Just make sure that he's all right," he said about Raul. "If you need anything, give me a call."

***

On the north side, Raul and Toya lived in the same apartment Toya had moved into after separating from Donnie. It was in an apartment complex near the upscale downtown of Milwaukee. Raul and Toya had the appearance of respectability—they dressed well, drove new whips, and gave off an aura of successful entrepreneurs. The only thing that didn't add up for their neighbors were the stressed-out lowlifes who were seen going in and out of the apartment at all hours of the day and night.

Raul and Toya did indeed have a major enterprise in mind. Between the two of them, they had cleared $2.5 million in less than six months from the frenetic pace of their drug deals. Much of the money had come from the pounds of marijuana they had moved. Once the weed had been sold, they were ready to invest the entire $2.5 million wad into the purchase of a ton of cocaine from Manuel, the connection Raul had made through Peso.

They made a trip to Miami to work out the cocaine deal. On the first trip, Peso joined them in Daytona Beach and drove with them to visit Manuel in Miami. Manuel invited them to his palatial estate.

"I'm happy you all could make it," Manuel said as he greeted the trio, who were seated on the imported furniture in the living room of his mansion.

"We wouldn't miss out on an opportunity to do more business with you," Peso said.

"Good. Because thus far, business with you has been going well." Manuel waved over a maid and requested a bottle of Dom P. He turned his attention to Raul. "I'm looking forward to doing business with you also. All I expect is for you to come with your money right."

"Money isn't a *problema*," Raul assured him.

Toya spoke up. "And all we expect is for you to make sure the product is quality."

"I like a feisty woman," Manuel said, wearing a grin. "You have nothing to worry about. I have some of the best quality product in the world."

"Good to know," said Raul.

The maid returned with the bottle of bubbly and some glasses. She poured drinks and passed them around before moving along to fulfill her duties.

Manuel took a swig from his glass. "You can stay here until you're ready to return home."

"We 'preciate the hospitality, Manuel," Peso said.

"Of course. *Mi casa su casa.* Make yourselves at home. I have a few things to handle tonight, but we have a big day ahead of us tomorrow." Manuel asked the maid to show his visitors to the guest rooms. He wanted them to be as comfortable as possible while in town. Having them as part of his operations would be good for business.

The next day, Manuel took them to visit a cocaine "factory" the Colombian trafficker was overseeing deep in the swamps. It was Raul's deal, but Peso went along for the ride. Peso knew that Manuel had tons and tons of cocaine but had never seen so many kilos all at once. The "factory" consisted of sheds with corrugated iron roofs and large tents spread over about an acre of swamp clearing. Even in the fall, the swamp was as humid as a steam bath, and the air was abuzz with mosquitoes.

People working near vats and barrels of chemicals paid little attention to the visitors as Manuel guided them through the production labyrinth step by step. Everywhere was the telltale odor of acetone.

Peso and Raul, both dressed expensively in designer clothes and absorbed by the complexity of the operation, asked questions.

Toya was impressed by the cleanliness, the organization, and the attention to the smallest detail. Though it was a shanty-village in the heart of the swamp that could be torn down and moved if necessary; the dirt streets were litter-free. A water truck made the rounds, sprinkling the bare earth to keep the dust under control.

Manuel showed them a ton of cocaine. It was stored inside a tent near what appeared to be the main building. Workers had already wrapped the cocaine into kilogram bricks and piled them inside wooden crates. The bricks had letters or symbols written on them with permanent markers. The crates were stacked on pallets. Nearby, there was a forklift.

The Colombian picked up a clear plastic bag full of cocaine from a bench and scooped out a couple of ounces into another bag. He handed it to his visitors as a sample. They snorted some on the spot. There were grunts and groans of approval.

Instead of shipping the cocaine through Peso's runners, Raul and Toya made arrangements with a Colombian named Herrera, the thin-faced scion of a trafficking family in Miami, to ship the load from Florida. Herrera's crew was connected to Manuel's organization.

Raul and Toya entered Manuel's restaurant and found Herrera seated at a table alone. They approached him and occupied the empty seats.

"So, Manuel told me that you're in need of my services," Herrera said.

"He told you right," Raul replied. "We need you to traffic a load to Milwaukee for us."

"And we're willing to pay you good," Toya added.

Herrera sipped from his glass of gin. "Since you're dealing with Manuel, I'll run the load for you. My sister, who lives in Miami, will receive the load, and I'll escort it to Milwaukee after taking charge of it in Miami."

"Sounds like a plan," Raul agreed.

The plan was for Herrera to drive to Milwaukee and be met by Raul and Toya at the Fiserv Forum. As soon as Herrera's sister got the load in Miami, they would expect Herrera to make the trip to Milwaukee. Once the cocaine shipment arrived at a stash house in Milwaukee, they would take possession of it, break it down into smaller loads, and run it to customers they had already lined up.

Before leaving Florida, Raul and Toya had another discussion with Manuel to work out further details of the deal. They visited the swamp factory one more time and saw the cocaine they would receive being packaged and marked "RT," signifying Raul and Toya.

On the way back to Milwaukee, they flew to Atlanta to work out details of a money-laundering scheme with a tall, distinguished-looking white banker who spoke with a British accent. When they returned, they calculated, they were going to quadruple their investment.

But things were not destined to go as planned.

Chapter 15

"After we get rid of this load, then we'll return to Miami and see Manuel. This time around, we'll double our load," Raul said.

"We will be set for life. No more worries forever. None," Toya responded.

Raul pulled the Porsche truck to a stop at a red light on 27th and North Street. "All we have to do is stay off the DEA's radar, and we'll be able to stay in business for a long time."

The couple was on their way to their downtown apartment after collecting funds from their workers. Over the past month, Raul and Toya's business had been going exceptionally well. Through their north side operation, they had already been able to move two separate loads of cocaine. Thus far, Manuel respected their ability to move so much product. In between doing business with the couple and Peso, Manuel was getting richer than ever before. However, Raul and Toya couldn't move as much product without the help of Peso and his connect—not only with the Colombian but also with the Milwaukee Drug Task Force. Raul knew it was best to contribute to the hustle fee, but Toya didn't think they should cut him in on their business affairs.

Once arriving at their complex, Raul circled the block twice just to be sure they weren't being tailed by Twelve or opps. Lately, he had been more cautious about someone tailing them. Maybe it was just his mind playing tricks on him now that they were getting money hand over fist. Toya tried convincing him that he was just being paranoid.

He parked the whip in front of the building, and she grabbed the tote bag filled with money before they stepped. Then the two made their way inside and headed up to their apartment, where they would count up the paper.

While Toya placed the stacks of cash on the kitchen table along with a money counter machine, Raul set out some lines of coke for them to indulge in. With so many bricks of pure cocaine coming in from their connect, they were able to feed their habit. But they needed to guard their habit before it consumed them.

Toya started admiring the crisp bills. She picked up a bundle and fanned through it absentmindedly.

"Damn, Raul, it's crazy to think we sittin' on this much paper," Toya said with a sly grin, stacking another bundle onto the table.

"Yeah, it's crazy all right, but I told you to stop leaving the money out. We gotta bag that shit up soon as we count it," Raul said, glancing over as he cut a few lines of coke.

Toya shrugged him off and kept stacking. "I'll get to it. Let me just count up real quick and—"

"Damn, Toya. You don't listen, do you?" Raul snapped, shaking his head as he took a bump off the counter.

"I really don't like how you talk to me sometimes. It's not as if the money's gonna grow legs and run away."

"Toya, put the fuckin' money in the bag like I told you to," Raul insisted. He was annoyed by the fact that she kept leaving the stacks of cash on the table after they had already counted them.

"Don't come at me like I'm some stupid *pendejo!*" Toya snapped back.

Raul scoffed. "Then why don't you stop actin' like one."

In the heat of the moment, Toya threw a paper bag full of money at Raul. He threw it back, hitting her above the eye. They began shoving each other.

"Raul, I'm tired of you putting your damn hands on me!" Toya grabbed her pistol, aimed at Raul's head, and pulled the trigger.

Click.

Toya had not chambered a round and had accidentally released the ammunition clip. Raul did not give her a second chance. He put his pistol to her head.

"Bitch, do you want to see how it feels to die?" he snarled.

Toya thought about her nine-year-old son, who was playing on the landing of the apartment, and silently prayed that he didn't happen to walk in on them. The boy wasn't aware of what was going on between Raul and his mom.

Raul got a hold of himself and threw down the pistol he had been holding to Toya's head.

"You lucky I'ma let your ass live. Don't you ever pull no fuckin' gun on me again," Raul forewarned. "Now let's get back to countin' this money."

While their business venture seemingly was on firm ground, Raul and Toya's personal relationship had begun to deteriorate. The arguments—frequently disagreements over business—were becoming daily occurrences. They both were snorting a lot of powder, making the arguments potentially dangerous.

After that nearly fatal argument, Raul and Toya realized they needed to cut down on their coke consumption. But their relationship would never again be the same.

During one of her trips to the south side to drop off some product to a worker, Toya took the opportunity to meet up with Peso at Lu's. They were seated at the bar, and Peso ordered them drinks. She felt the need to talk with him about Raul.

"I see business on the north side has been goin' well for you and Raul lately," Peso pointed out.

Toya let out a breath. "Yeah, it has. But our relationship hasn't been as successful lately."

"What's been the problem? Seems to me everything is just fine."

"We argue and fight about a lot. Sometimes I think I'm not the woman Raul wants." She sipped her bottle of Corona.

"Toya, take it from me, every relationship has their problems. It can't be that bad."

"But it is, Peso," Toya rebutted. She shifted towards him on her stool. "Just the other day he and I got into an altercation and I drew my gun on him and pulled the trigger. Luckily, I had not chambered a round and had accidentally released the ammunition clip, or it would have been a different story."

Peso was taken aback by what she had just told him. He could see in her tearful eyes that it hurt her that things with Raul had gotten to such a point. "You're probably the only person who's ever gotten that close to killin' him and lived to tell about it," Peso admitted.

"I know, right." She herself knew that Raul was capable of murder at any given moment, so she was lucky he had not taken her life that night. "Peso, I just want things with Raul to work out. He's a good man and I do love him. However, our relationship and business doesn't mesh well. He wants things a certain way, and I disagree."

"Then y'all have to find ways to compromise."

"But you know how adamant Raul can be."

"Yeah, I do. I'll talk with him about it. You just keep him in line as best as you can."

Toya sighed. "I'll try my best."

***

Toya called Miami in regard to their shipment. When a woman answered, Toya politely asked, "Has the 'girl' been sent?"

"Yes, the 'girl' has already left," said the woman, who was Herrera's sister. "She should be there by tomorrow."

"Thanks."

Raul and Toya were expecting their third load from Manuel by way of Herrera. Even though their relationship was rocky, they were still in business, and there was still money to be made.

The next day, before meeting with Herrera at the drop-off location, Raul, Toya, and Toya's nine-year-old son drove to the south side and checked into a motel in preparation for a busy day. Among the tasks on their list, they had to collect $150,000 from a heroin dealer on the south side and then make a heroin delivery to another customer. Afterward, they planned to meet with Herrera near Fiserv Forum to collect the shipment from Florida.

Raul and Toya decided to drive to the stash house to wrap up some business with Peso, then head to the location where the cocaine had been delivered. Inside the stash house, they sat on the couch in the living room. Chato, Paulie, and Felix were present. Raul did most of the talking with Peso.

"Peso, we have another load that needs to be moved. And we'll need you to make sure the DTF doesn't intervene."

"As long as the hustle fee is paid, then you don't have to be concerned about Captain Danielson," Peso assured him.

"On top of the usual percentage of the hustle fee, we'll pay you an additional fifty Gs for bein' able to move our product," Raul proffered.

"Sounds good."

Just after returning to their downtown apartment, Raul and Toya got into another argument and began shouting at each other. They had been snorting coke, and it was fueling their anger. They were discussing the deal with Peso.

"Raul, I agree with you on every aspect of the deal except for one—whether or not to cut in Peso. I don't think we should have to give him additional money even though we're not going through Peso's organization," she objected.

"With me, it's a matter of loyalty," Raul replied.

"And with me, it's strictly business. Why pay for protection that we're not even going to use?"

"Toya, if it wasn't for Peso, then we wouldn't even be in the position we're in. Plus, he's always been there for us."

"Don't get me wrong. I know Peso is a good guy, but you don't owe him your life," she insisted.

Raul stepped out of the apartment to cool off. He usually carried a gun with him wherever he went. For some reason, he had left his .45 in the Porsche. He stepped up to the vehicle and was about to open it when a swarm of DEA agents and city policemen moved in to arrest him.

DEA agents shoved him to his knees. One of the agents ordered him to lie face down on the ground. It was cold outside, and Raul was already kneeling in a puddle of water.

"Hit the position—face down!" the agent repeated.

Raul looked at him with contempt and said, "You know who the fuck you're talkin' to?"

The agent shoved the muzzle of an M-14 to the back of Raul's head and pushed until Raul's face was pressed into the puddle.

"Yeah, I know who you are," the DEA agent said.

A surveillance team had been following Raul and Toya from the north side to the expressway, but the officers dared not follow too closely for fear of giving themselves away. It was the expressway Raul and Toya always took south. Instead of trailing them, the surveillance team waited along a side street to see if Raul and Toya would return. Sure enough, a day later, the brand-new black Porsche truck that Raul and Toya were driving reappeared. And it was time to bust them.

***

"What do you mean they were arrested?"

"Word is, they were taken into custody last night."

Peso was on a call with Paulie, who had reported to him that Raul and Toya had been snatched up by the DEA.

"I need you to find out what their charges are. And try to get word to them that I have their backs," Peso ordered. As much as he trusted the two, he wanted to make sure neither of them would turn on him.

"Will do," Paulie said.

Peso ended the call. He lay back in bed with Mona beside him as his mind raced. *I warned Raul this would happen,* he thought.

It turned out Peso had been right about the dangers of running a narcotics operation on the north side. Only a short while after they began operating out of the downtown apartment, the police were on to them. Police informants had not only identified Raul and Toya as significant drug traffickers but also as high-ranking members of Peso's trafficking organization. This brought even greater police scrutiny.

Even worse, the informants stated that Raul had bragged about killing people for Peso—among them, two young men who were shot to death at the trap spot on 6th and Beecher Street. Just as Peso had predicted, the police began tailing Raul and Toya, gathering intel on their movements, and looking for a crack in their operation.

The police subpoenaed cellphone company records for Toya's number and found countless long-distance calls placed to Mexico, Chicago, Detroit, Des Moines, and Miami. Many of the numbers turned out to belong to suspected drug traffickers. A state judge authorized a wiretap on Toya's cellphone and even bugged her apartment.

When Raul and Toya were close to killing each other, Milwaukee police and DEA agents sat sweating inside a van parked outside, listening in on their bugged argument. What were they supposed to do? If they rushed into the apartment to stop somebody from getting killed, they'd blow their surveillance. But when it really sounded like Raul was about to kill Toya, her nine-year-old son, who was playing on the landing of the apartment, became their concern. The agents decided to grab the boy to get him out of harm's way. Just as the agents jumped out of the van, however, Raul got ahold of himself and threw down the pistol he had been holding to Toya's head.

Through their eavesdropping, the authorities soon learned that a major cocaine deal was in the works. The language Raul and Toya used was vague and coded, leaving the police guessing at the details. Still, the wiretap picked up Toya's optimism and a hint of the size of the transaction.

Later, the authorities realized they had acted too quickly. If they had continued their surveillance for just a few more days, they could've caught Raul, Toya, and Herrera with a major load of cocaine.

Raul and Toya were arraigned in Milwaukee district court and charged with twelve felony counts, ranging from racketeering to conspiracy to traffic cocaine and heroin. Raul was later arraigned in federal court for possession of an enhanced weapon.

Toya hired an attorney and was able to get out on bond, but the bond and attorney fees were expensive, leaving her financially wiped out. The $2.5 million she and Raul had raised over the previous six months was still in Miami, and she figured she would never see it again. She had to start making money all over again.

In desperation, Toya drove to the south side to see Peso about getting fronted some loads of marijuana. Peso cleared out Lu's Bar & Grille so they could talk, just like he had the first time she came to meet him. Peso sent his cousin to fetch drinks from the bar, and the cousin returned with glasses of Patrón. Peso's shooters stood watch at the front and back doors. Peso had been eager to find out what went wrong ever since he heard about the arrest.

"So, what's goin' on, Toya?" Peso asked.

"I need to make money, and I need to make money fast," Toya told him.

"First, I need to know some things. How did the DEA catch on to y'all? And how did you manage to get out of jail and not Raul?" Peso asked, taking a swig from his glass of Patrón.

"I was allowed out on bond because I wasn't considered a flight risk. But the court was certain Raul would skip out of the country if he were set free, so he was denied bond. As for our arrest, it happened because a bunch of people snitched on us," Toya explained. "Milwaukee police developed four informants who gave them a wealth of information about me and Raul—and also about our ties to you."

Peso peered at her, perplexed. "How do you know I was brought up in your case?"

"I brought this along for you to see for yourself."

Toya reached inside her expensive Birkin handbag and pulled out a copy of a twenty-nine-page wiretap affidavit. Milwaukee authorities had presented it to a district court judge to get an extension on the original wiretap authorization, which had gone on for a month. The document summarized intelligence gathered from the informants, who were not identified by name. She handed the paperwork to Peso.

Between sips of Patrón and long drags on his Backwood stuffed with weed, Peso read the entire document, pausing to ask Toya to explain things he didn't understand. They tried to deduce who the informants were and came up with several possibilities. Peso never said what he was going to do about them. All he told Toya was, "Don't worry about it," and he kept the document.

"Now, let's get down to business. What can I do for you?"

"I want a load of marijuana. I have some customers who'll buy as much weed as I can supply, but I don't have a dime to my name anymore," Toya told him.

All of her vehicles had been confiscated. The only vehicle remaining was the SUV with a trap compartment she had left with Peso before her arrest. Peso had recently sent the SUV off with a load, and it wasn't back yet. This meant Peso would have to give her the load on credit and provide her with a vehicle equipped with a trap compartment.

"When are you gonna need it?" Peso asked.

"Right now. I need it now."

"Do you have somebody to drive?"

"No, I'll drive it myself."

"I don't want you to get caught. I'll give you a driver," Peso said.

"I don't have money to pay a driver," Toya replied. "Every dime I had went to those attorneys. So I'd rather do it myself."

"I'll pay the driver," Peso said. "When do you want to go?"

"Tomorrow."

***

The next day, Toya loaded up the trap compartment of an SUV with one hundred pounds of weed at one of Peso's stash houses. The driver assigned by Peso drove the SUV across town and took it to the destination Toya had specified. She collected the payment and returned to the south side with Peso's share of the money.

Over the next couple of weeks, she moved four loads, making a quick twenty-five bands each time. But the money vanished almost as fast as she made it, eaten up by attorney fees. To her despair, her expensive legal help was not getting her anywhere. Her case took a turn for the worse when one of her former runners agreed to testify against her and Raul. Toya could see the writing on the wall: she was going to spend at least the next ten years in jail. Her only option was fleeing to Mexico—an alternative that didn't even appeal to her. Her welfare and security in Mexico would depend almost entirely on Peso, and she was not sure Peso was going to last much longer as the drug lord within the Mexican Cartel.

Every time she saw him, she noted the effects of his growing cocaine addiction. The last time she was with him he mumbled a lot, and it was just hard to understand him. He kept repeating himself. It just was not the same alert, commanding, sharp-as-a-whip Peso that she had met after Donnie's arrest. Someone in his condition could not remain in power indefinitely.

Even before that meeting, Toya had been toying with the idea of plea bargaining with the District Attorney in Milwaukee for a lighter sentence. She was exhausted by the life she'd been living. Her existence felt like a vicious cycle: hustling to make money by trafficking drugs to pay attorneys to get her off the hook for trafficking. It was a loop leading nowhere but the grave—or prison. She couldn't shake the feeling that her life was slipping away. If she hadn't been arrested, she would likely still be with Raul and Peso, dodging bullets in one of their inevitable shootouts. And if she happened to be with Peso when things went down, she knew she might not survive.

The day after that last visit with Peso, Toya drove to the courthouse to see about entering a guilty plea. As it turned out, the Milwaukee authorities and the DEA considered her an important drug operative and potential source of information.

In what seemed like a boardroom inside the courthouse, Toya and her attorney sat on the opposite side of a huge oakwood table from the District Attorney and the DEA agent heading her case. She didn't know what the outcome of this particular meeting would be, but she hoped for the best— without having to do the worst. Her attorney assured her that he would negotiate an agreement with the authorities that would have her walk, but she didn't know exactly what position he would put her in.

"Ms. Miller, are you aware of the serious nature of your charges?" the District Attorney, a middle-aged white woman, asked Toya, addressing her formally.

Toya looked to her attorney, who gave her a slight nod. "Yes, I'm aware," she said.

"And given the seriousness you could end up in prison for a very long time. However, we want to offer you an opportunity to be on the right side of the law and help us in our case."

"And what will my client be expected to do?" Toya's well-dressed attorney inquired.

"For starters," the DEA agent piped in, "we'll expect her to admit to all of the crimes she has committed and provide a full debrief on them."

"And if she is willing to do so, then we may be able to reach a mutual agreement on her sentence," the DA added.

Toya looked perplexed. "That's all I'll be expected to do? I won't have to implicate anyone else?"

"Well, not exactly," the DA said. "You will have to inform us of everyone who was with you during these crimes."

"Also, we'll expect you to give up Lupe "Peso" Martinez," the DEA agent told her.

That last part didn't sit well with Toya. She never wanted to say or do anything to bring down others, especially Peso. But she had to think about her nine-year-old son. Was she willing to be out of his life for many years instead of just working a deal? She knew what she signed up for; she just didn't think it would come to this.

"No. I won't give up Peso," Toya said flatly.

The DA seemed frustrated with Toya's response. "Ms. Miller, why protect a lowlife who has done nothing but put you and the entire city in grave danger?" she spat. "You're making a big mistake here, Ms. Miller," the DA warned.

"Believe it or not, Peso was always good to me. Besides, he won't just surrender."

"You just leave that part to us," The DEA agent rejoined. "All you'll have to do is lure him in for us."

"I already told you that I won't do it. I don't think that's the way he should be killed, not Peso. Not by a woman," Toya told the authorities.

The attorney felt it necessary to speak up: "Listen, I'm sure all of this is too much for my client to take in at once. How about you all give her time to think things through?"

For Toya, though, there was nothing to think through. She just wouldn't give up Peso, even if that meant having to do some time in prison.

***

Days Later—
Eventually, an agreement was reached. Toya was granted immunity from prosecution for each and every crime she had ever committed, provided she admit to the crime and go into detail about it. In exchange for a probated sentence after pleading guilty to the trafficking charges, she agreed to cooperate in investigations stemming from the information she provided.

The only thing she refused to do for the authorities was set up Peso. DEA agents asked her to lay out a plan to lure him to the north side of the city. It would not have been too difficult, she knew. All she would have to do would be to arrange for a big load of marijuana to come across at the 27th Street bridge, then fake breakdown on the north side of the city—just like not long ago when the SUV broke down and the two pack boys had to trek back to Milwaukee on the expressway to fetch help. Peso would surely form an expedition to recover the SUV.

But Toya refused. She knew that Peso would never surrender; he would never allow Milwaukee police to take him alive. If anything, he'd show up with a small army of his men—Chato, Paulie, Felix, and his nameless shooters—armed to the teeth with machine guns and boxes of ammo. The resulting clash would be the biggest shootout the city had ever seen, with blood and bodies everywhere. That would be Peso's parting style. She believed that Peso was going to die a violent death—probably sooner rather than later. But she did not want to be the one to bring it about.

Chapter 16

Tamera placed plates of food in front of Peso and Chato, who were seated at her kitchen table. As always, she was happy to have her son visit her, especially since he had brought her nephew along.

"This looks good, Ma," Peso commented, eyeing the food on his plate. Chicken fajitas and a side dish of Spanish rice sat steaming before him.

"Yeah, Tía, I can't wait to dig in," Chato added.

Tamera poured them both glasses of iced water and set the pitcher on the table. "Just make sure you enjoy," she insisted.

"I'm sure I will, Tía," Chato replied.

Tamera turned her attention to Peso. "So, how have things been going?"

"Things are alright," Peso replied nonchalantly, scooping a spoonful of rice into his mouth.

"No, son. I mean, how are things *really* going? And please don't give me any more baseless answers."

Peso paused, peering at his mother for a moment. He set down his spoon. "Keepin' it real with you, Ma, things haven't been goin' exactly how I want. Between the arrests and the beefs, I don't know what to expect."

"Lupe, that reminds me of what your dad went through," Tamera said. "And like him, the best advice I can offer you is to get out of that lifestyle before it's too late."

"Ma, it's already too late."

"No, it's not. You still have time to get out and do something different with your life, unlike your dad and brother, whose time has come and gone. You think I want to bury you next?" Tamera's voice cracked with emotion. "You have a family of your own to think about, Lupe. You should care about being here for Mona and Maxine in this lifetime."

After losing her husband Luis and their son Juan to the streets, Tamera was constantly worried Peso would be next. She desperately wanted him to break the cycle and be there for his girlfriend Mona and their daughter Maxine.

"Believe me, Ma, I want to be here for them too. And that's why I ain't about to let someone do me like they did Dad or Juan," Peso told her.

"You can't control that, Lupe. I'm sure neither of them thought someone would take them out, but things happen in that lifestyle that you can't control. I don't like the thought of losing you, but I know it's a possibility. And I'm even more worried about your cousin always being with you," she said, glancing at Chato.

"Tía, I appreciate you bein' concerned, but there's no need for you to worry," Chato piped in. "I got Lupe's back, and he's got mine."

"And what if that isn't enough?" Tamera challenged.

"Ma, I understand your concerns. Just know I'll always keep what you said in mind to stay vigilant," Peso assured her.

***

After parting from Tamera's place, Peso and Chato drove through traffic, heading to one of the stash spots. They rode in Chato's whip as Baby Money's track "Chances Make Champions" played softly in the background.

Peso couldn't shake his mother's words. Her concerns cut deep. She wasn't wrong—his father and brother had lost their lives to the lifestyle. Countless others had too. And Peso didn't want that fate for himself or Chato. *Damn, Mom is right*, he thought. *But I gotta do what I gotta do.*

"Cuz, you thinkin' 'bout what Tía said to you?" Chato asked, noticing Peso's quiet demeanor.

Peso nodded slowly. "Yeah. She's right about how we live. I don't want neither of us to go out like the others."

"Listen, Peso, if we ever have to go out, then we'll go out in a blaze of glory," Chato declared.

"Facts." Peso shifted in his seat, turning toward Chato. "Shit's been crazy in the streets lately. Raul and Toya gettin' arrested let me know Twelve is watchin' close."

"You think Toya's still good for business?" Chato asked.

"Don't know. We'll have to see what's goin' on with Raul first. I tried tellin' his ass not to open up shop on the damn north side in the first place. But if I find out she's workin' with the feds, I'm gonna smoke that bitch," Peso vowed.

"Say no more," Chato replied as he braked the car at a stoplight near the 27th Street bridge.

"We still got money to make. I got another load comin' soon, but since all my other runners are busy, I'm gonna need someone to bring the next load to me," Peso said.

"I'm sure you can find one of the young'uns who wanna prove themselves."

"You right. And I know just the one."

"Just make sure whoever the nigga is can handle pressure in case somethin' goes wrong," Chato advised.

Suddenly, an SUV pulled up beside them, and a lone gunman leaned halfway out of the window. Peso peeped the shooter just as he extended his firearm out the driver's window at their whip.

"Duck, Chato! Duck!" Peso shouted.

Ack, ack, ack, ack, ack, ack!

Antonio—a young Mexican man with curly black hair and a penchant for murder—had been hired to kill Peso. He fired numerous rounds at the whip while they waited at the light. Miraculously, the shots missed. Antonio sped off, but Chato and Peso gave chase.

As they tore down residential streets, Peso could have fired back but held off, afraid of hitting innocent kids. The chase led to a factory on the outskirts of the neighborhood. Antonio's SUV barreled over a speed bump and into the nearly empty parking lot. Chato followed, bouncing over the bump with the shooter's vehicle just ahead. Peso leaned out the window, gripping an assault rifle with one arm.

Boc, boc, boc, boc, boc!

The ride was bumpy, but Peso never missed. He was sure he hit Antonio because the would-be assassin veered off and crashed into a tree. He and Chato thought Antonio was dead or mortally wounded, but just as they jumped out of their whip, Antonio popped up from behind his crashed SUV and fired more rounds.

Antonio had another pistol. And when he used up his ammunition, Chato ran around one side, and Peso ran around the other side of the SUV. The SUV was idling at an angle and the shooter was lying against the seat trying to reload. But they didn't give him a chance. Antonio's hands were shaking severely as he frantically tried to reload the blick. Peso and Chato aimed their rifles and fired into the hitman's back until they ran out of ammunition, shooting him to death.

Antonio slumped lifelessly against the seat.

They hurried back to the whip and smashed off.

"Dawg, who the fuck was that nigga?" Chato asked as he sped down the street.

"I'ont even know. But I'm sure the nigga was sent by Junior to slide on me," Peso hissed through clenched teeth.

Chato swerved around a vehicle, gripping the wheel tightly. "We gotta get Junior's bitch-ass out the way."

"And we will, Peso replied firmly."

***

After the shootout, instead of heading to one of the stash spots as originally planned, Peso had Chato drop him off at Sierra's place. She was expecting him, since he had called ahead to let her know that he was on the way. Sierra waited for him at the entrance of her apartment complex. She had been on her way to bed, wearing a pair of Chanel slides and a silk robe, her hair tied back in a messy bun.

When they reached her apartment, Sierra led Peso upstairs. Once inside, he peeled off his Chrome Hearts hoodie and tossed it over the arm of the couch. He pulled the Glock from his waistband and set it on the end table, then leaned back into the cushions with a heavy sigh. Sierra, perceptive as always, could tell something was weighing on him. She had sensed it from the tone of his voice on the phone.

"So, what's the matter with you, Peso?" Sierra inquired. She reached over and grabbed a half-smoked blunt out the ashtray on the coffee table and lit it up.

"It's all the shit goin' on in the streets. If it ain't Twelve tryin' to take me down, then it's a opp tryin' to take me out," Peso heatedly expressed.

"Don't tell me that someone else tried to take your life."

"That's exactly what I'm tellin' you." He scoffed. "And I'ma make sure the one who's behind it get his."

"Peso"—she passed him the blunt—"maybe you need to lay low for a while. It seems to be too much heat on you and your people at the moment."

"As much as I would like to, I can't do that right now, Sierra. I still have business to take of in these streets," he told her.

Sierra scooted closer to him and palmed his cheek. "Just don't let your business and the streets be the only things you care about. There's more to life."

"I understand. Believe me, I care about you more than that shit."

He loved Mona but there was something about being with Sierra that made him feel good about her presence. Without any further words, Peso kissed Sierra's lips. The way he felt about her was different from his feelings for Mona.

He helped Sierra out of her silk robe, then her bra and panties, and she returned the favor, removing his clothes piece by piece. Peso pushed her back on the couch, planting kisses on her lips, down her neck, and over her collarbone, trailing lower and over her tummy until his face was between her legs. Shivering, she loved the warm feel of his mouth on her pussy as he orally pleased her.

"Dammit, baby, your mouth feels so good on this pussy," Sierra moaned. Her back arched and she spread her legs wide, allowing him full access to her wetness. The way he licked all over her pussy lips and finger-fucked her felt so tantalizing. "Mmmm . . . I love it so much!" she gasped, gripping the couch cushions.

Peso spat on her pussy, then stroked his forefinger and middle finger rapidly back and forth in her. "This pussy is so wet, Sie," he said in a lowered, gruff voice. After a moment, he removed his fingers, then returned to orally pleasuring her, flicking his tongue over her swollen clitoris. He slurped and licked and sucked on her pussy until she reached climax, her cum oozing in his mouth.

"Oooh, yesss!" Sierra couldn't hold back her release.

"Damn, this pussy tastes yummy, my baby."

Peso sat back on the couch and Sierra straddled his lap. She grabbed his hard dick and guided it inside of her wet-shot, loving the feeling of him sliding deep within her. Peso grasped Sierra's ass cheeks as she bounced on his dick.

"Uhhh, shit, Peso," Sierra groaned, throwing her head back as her pussy tightened around his dick. Peso stood up with her in his arms, slamming her back and forth onto his dick, driving deeper with every thrust.

"Oohhh, my-fuckin'-goodness!" Sierra shouted, her voice trembling with ecstasy.

"You like how I beat this pussy up, don't you?" Peso bragged.

"Yeeessss, I do!" she cried. She came again, clawing at his bare back as she climaxed. Her warm cum juices flowed down his inner thighs as her body shook with pleasure.

Peso planted her on the floor, then she knelt before him and took his hardness in her mouth. While looking up at him, she spat on the dick and licked all over it, from the sac to its tip. He watched with pleasure while Sierra used both hands to stroke his stick as she sucked it as if her life depended on it. He palmed her head and began fuckin' her pretty mouth, causing her to gag some as the tip of his dick met her tonsils. But that only turned her on more and encouraged her to orally please him even better.

"Fuck, babygirl . . . I'm finna bust a nut," Peso grunted. His knees began buckling from the blow job. It wasn't long before he released his semen all down her throat and some on her lips that she licked up.

Afterward, they lay cuddled on the couch, Sierra resting her head on Peso's chest. But Peso's mind was elsewhere, racing through the chaos of his life. Between his love life and his street life, he just wanted to live his best life. But deep down, he knew his days might be numbered.

Chapter 17

At a tollbooth between Wisconsin and Illinois, state patrol officers had found the location ideal for catching drivers with expired licenses, broken taillights, missing vehicle registration documents, failure to wear seat belts, or other minor infractions. Just by spending an hour there per shift, a trooper could issue stacks of citations. Occasionally, they even nabbed drunk drivers or car thieves.

On this particular day, Sergeant James, a twelve-year veteran of the state police, was manning the tollbooth with another trooper when a blue SUV with tinted windows approached. As the SUV rolled forward, it suddenly stalled.

The driver, a Hispanic teenager, restarted the SUV, but as soon as he put it into gear, it stalled again.

"May I see your driver's license?" James asked, stepping closer to the vehicle. The young man, flustered but polite, began fishing through his wallet. Meanwhile, James glanced inside the SUV and noticed that the 'oil' light was on.

"Your vehicle will run better if you put some oil in it," James commented.

"Thanks," the teenager replied politely.

James studied the driver closely. He looked clean-cut, friendly, and relaxed. Nothing in his demeanor suggested he was hiding anything. Perhaps he was just inexperienced or clueless about vehicle maintenance.

The teenager rummaged through his wallet for a moment, then began searching the glove compartment for the vehicle's registration but came up empty-handed. "I think I left them at home," he admitted.

"Mind if I ask where you're headed?" James inquired.

"I was on my way to visit my mother in Kenosha, a small town in southeastern Wisconsin," the teen explained. "She's in the hospital after a bad car accident. I found out when I got off work and borrowed this SUV because my car wasn't running right." He introduced himself as Leo Reyes, a nineteen-year-old, and said the SUV belonged to his wife's brother. The SUV had a Wisconsin dealer's tag on the rear window with the address of a Milwaukee dealership, suggesting it had been recently purchased.

James checked the dealer tag's identification number against the vehicle identification number (VIN) on the dashboard. The numbers didn't match. After jotting down the tag number, he walked around the SUV and carefully examined the gas tank. He noticed it had been freshly painted.

Just then, James' partner, Sergeant Jeffrey York, approached after issuing a ticket to another motorist. "What do you have?" York asked.

"He doesn't have a driver's license. The tag doesn't belong to this SUV. And there's something off about this gas tank," James explained.

"What do you mean?" York asked.

James had recently spoken with a state patrolman in Zion, Illinois, who had busted a false gas tank containing marijuana. He suspected they might have stumbled upon something similar. York stepped to the rear of the SUV and tapped the gas tank. He then opened the fuel valve, causing a jet of gas to spew out.

Since things seemed suspicious, the officers dug deeper. None of Leo Reyes' stories checked out. The Milwaukee dealership didn't exist. No one matching the description of his mother had been involved in a car accident in Kenosha, nor was anyone with her name admitted to any hospital in the area. In fact, there hadn't been a traffic accident in or around Kenosha in over a week.

"You're coming with us," James told the driver.

As much as Leo wanted to flee, he knew he wouldn't get far. Peso had instructed all his runners: if it looks like you're going to get caught with a load, drop everything and run. If you can't run, surrender. Peso could always post bail. He just didn't want law enforcement killings bringing heat down on his organization.

Leo Reyes followed the troopers for several miles up I-94 to a quiet Wisconsin town. They arrived at a car dealership's service shop, where a mechanic slid under the SUV to unbolt the gas tank. York, who was built like a linebacker, strained as he tried to lift the tank but couldn't budge it.

"Hey, there's gotta be another bolt under here. I can't move this thing," York said.

The mechanic slid back under. "No, there's no other bolt."

York kept lifting and tugging until he finally managed to dislodge the tank and pull it out from beneath the SUV. By then, a magistrate and his secretary had arrived, as the officers had radioed ahead to request a search warrant. Once the warrant was signed, they began examining the gas tank. It wasn't long before they spotted a thin line of sanded Bondo. Using a hammer and chisel, they punched out a rectangular plate.

James and York had expected to find marijuana, but when York reached inside and pulled out a plastic-wrapped package marked with the letter "P," he immediately knew it wasn't weed. Slicing the package open, he revealed white crystalline powder.

"Cocaine!" York exclaimed.

When the gas tank was finally emptied, they counted 111 tightly wrapped plastic containers, each holding about a kilogram of cocaine. The total haul weighed in at 246 pounds, with an estimated street value of fifty million dollars. It was one of the largest cocaine seizures in Wisconsin history and one of the biggest drug busts ever made on an American highway.

After the packages were removed, one of the officers read Leo Reyes his Miranda rights and placed him in handcuffs. Up until that moment, the young driver had behaved like someone with nothing to hide, even curling up in a corner of the garage to take a nap while the police searched the SUV. But as the trooper recited his rights, Leo suddenly burst into tears.

"Why don't you just take your gun out and kill me now?" he sobbed. "They're gonna kill me any-fuckin'-way."

The size of the load found in Leo Reyes' SUV was already a clear indication that Leo Reyes worked for a big smuggling ring. Investigators quickly grasped how well-organized the operation was when two high-profile criminal defense lawyers from Milwaukee showed up to represent the low-ranking courier—the expendable "cannon fodder" of drug distribution networks.

Four days later, the investigation moved to Milwaukee, where police found another drug cache in a red SUV parked in front of Leo Reyes' apartment. Like the first vehicle, this SUV also had a false gas tank bolted to the bottom. Inside, police officers found 263 pounds of cocaine in kilogram bricks with the same marking as the packaging found in the tollbooth bust. Neighbors informed police that at least three other SUVs with similar characteristics had been parked in front of the residence in the days prior.

Soon after the record-setting twin seizures, narcotics investigators from Miami called Milwaukee authorities to share information about a recent bust there. Two months before Leo Reyes' arrest, Miami police had seized 556 pounds of cocaine at a stash house in a suburb of Miami—a bust that had been one of the Florida's largest cocaine seizures at the time.

The Miami bust and the seizures in Milwaukee had notable similarities. In Miami, the cocaine had been transported in false gas tanks attached to SUVs with Wisconsin license plates. Investigators were left wondering: were these vehicles part of the same smuggling network? Most suspects arrested in the Miami case were Mexican nationals, with the rest being Colombian. Was this group an extension of the established Mexican-Colombian smuggling combines, or was it part of a new organization? And how did the Wisconsin license plates fit into the picture?

Two Milwaukee DEA agents began following up on leads culled from items confiscated at Leo Reyes' apartment, including cellphone bills, business cards, and scraps of paper. The investigation led them to a cabinet shop in a rundown redbrick neighborhood on Milwaukee's south side. One agent's pulse quickened when he peered through the shop window and spotted two false gas tanks, one of which had a hole cut into its side. Inside the shop, the agents found a piece of paper with scribbled notes and a hand-drawn map.

"Why, lookee here!" said the agent. "I think I can tell you right now who's behind all of this cocaine shit."

The map showed directions to a garage in small town east of Milwaukee. Paulie's cellphone number was scribbled above the map. Originally from Mexico, Paulie had become an American citizen and had been raised by his family in Milwaukee.

Posing as car owners looking for parts for a 1986 Chevy Caprice, the agents visited Paulie's garage and adjacent wrecking yard. While Paulie himself wasn't present, the workers—presumably Paulie's sons or nephews—allowed the agents to look around. During their visit, the agents spotted a false gas tank lying on the garage floor.

The investigation began to snowball. Customs agents in Milwaukee were conducting late-night meetings with an informant who had ties to Peso's organization. After being debriefed, the informant was sent back to Mexico. He told agents he had seen Paulie at one of Peso's stash houses during a cocaine shipment. The informant claimed to have witnessed the cocaine being stored and later distributed to prominent dealers. He also reported being present when Peso met with the DTF captain to pay the hustle fee.

Every time some drug-related activity took place, DTF officers were involved, the informant said.

It was one thing for an informant to have seen false gas tanks being loaded up with kilo bricks of cocaine in Milwaukee, but it was another to uncover evidence that would connect them to Leo Reyes. The informant could not recall seeing anyone matching the young courier's description. Nor could he recall the license plate numbers and other details of the SUVs he saw at Peso's places that would indisputably link the tollbooth, Milwaukee, and Miami cocaine loads to Peso.

Even so, the DEA agents were confident that they finally had an overview of the smuggling operation.

Evidence presented in federal court revealed that Leo Reyes worked for a Milwaukee-based smuggling network run by a Mexican national named Julio. Initially, investigators suspected Julio of working directly with Colombian cocaine producers and employing his own couriers. However, they later concluded that Julio was merely a subcontractor handling high-risk smuggling jobs for those with Colombian connections.

The real mastermind was Lupe "Peso" Martinez, the critical link in a supply chain that began in Colombia and ended at various delivery points across the United States.

It became clear that this was an enormous case with vast, distributing implications. Had the Colombians shifted their smuggling operations from Florida to Milwaukee? If so, Milwaukee stood to become the center of corruption and murder and drug wars.

The investigation had become too massive for the two DEA agents assigned to it. Each fresh lead brought new gold mines of information about Peso and hundreds of other people—from car thieves to heroin dealers—who did business with him.

The DEA chief in Milwaukee conferred with the chief prosecutor at the U.S. Attorney's office in Milwaukee. They agreed that the time had come to turn the Peso investigation into an Organized Crime Drug Enforcement Task Force (OCDETF) case.

The Reagan administration had created twelve regional OCDETFs to dismantle "high-level drug trafficking enterprises" through the prosecution of its most important members. Inspired by an earlier task force in south Florida, the idea was to combine narcotics investigators from various federal, state, and local law enforcement agencies into a single investigative unit.

A task force committee consisting of representatives of the DEA, the FBI, U.S. Customs, the Immigration and Naturalization Service, the Internal Revenue Service, the U.S. Attorney's office, the Milwaukee Police Department, and the Wisconsin Department of Public Safety jammed into the DEA's conference room in Milwaukee to discuss the Lupe "Peso" Martinez organization.

Copies of a five-page DEA assessment of Peso's organization were passed around. Then, Thompson, the silver-haired task force coordinator and senior DEA special agent in Milwaukee, addressed the group.

"The tentacles of this organization stretch across the Mexican states and deep into the U.S.," Thompson began. "Wisconsin, Texas, Illinois, Idaho, Michigan, Indiana, California, New York, and Colorado—all are impacted. Our current assessment identifies over 500 individuals connected to this network of family members, friends, and associates."

"Lupe "Peso" Martinez has been well documented as an extremely dangerous and ruthless fugitive who has been responsible, directly or indirectly, for more than twenty murders. Firearms are imported into Milwaukee from the other states by members of the Peso organization. As with stolen vehicles, these firearms most often exchanged for drugs . . ."

"Current intelligence indicates that numerous public officials throughout Milwaukee, which include police captains, local police officers, narcotic detectives, and other elected and appointed officials, are associates of the Peso organization. Seven or eight or local officials and cops from Milwaukee, Kenosha, and Racine counties were under suspicion," Thompson laid out.

Thompson's mention of local officials on Peso's payroll raised eyebrows around the room.

He continued, recounting the investigation's timeline—from Leo Reyes' arrest at the tollbooth to the discovery of the cocaine depot in Milwaukee. Thompson also outlined Peso's criminal history, from his truck stop heroin sting to his current marijuana, heroin, and cocaine operations.

"The task force's goal is to dismantle all known factions of Peso's organization and bring him to justice. Reports suggest that Peso occasionally crosses the border to visit family in Mexico, so he's a flight risk. Capturing him beforehand is critical," Thompson concluded.

Lupe "Peso" Martinez had been around for several years. Everyone in the room knew of him, and nearly everyone had dreamed at one time or another of capturing the drug lord. After nearly three hours of reports and discussion, the committee voted. It was a unanimous show of hands. Peso and his organization would be the next target for the task force.

Thompson looked into the eyes of the men in the room and stated, "We've known about this guy for a long time, and everyone feels that it is about time we went after him. Let's stop Lupe "Peso" Martinez—dead or alive."

To Be Continued...

ABOUT THE AUTHOR

Martell "Troublesome" Bolden is one of the hottest authors out in the field of street lit. Straight from the streets of Milwaukee, he grew up in an environment well-known for its drug trafficking and bloody murders, which he inevitably became a product of both. He has been incarcerated for nearly two decades, and will soon be released.

Troublesome writes from his personal experiences of living the street life. As an author, he aims to captivate and entertain the reader and evoke emotions through the power of storytelling. He is the author of some of the hottest urban fiction on the shelf, those titles include: TRAP GOD I, II & III; MONEY IN THE GRAVE I, II & III; RICH $AVAGE I, II & III, and CARTEL MONEY I & II.

Be on the lookout for more of the hottest street lit by Martell "Troublesome" Bolden coming soon...

Lock Down Publications and Ca$h Presents
Assisted Publishing Packages

Due to an increase in the price of services we have increased our prices. The prices below reflect the price increase as of 11/1/24.

BASIC PACKAGE	UPGRADED PACKAGE
$699	**$1000**
Editing	Typing
Cover Design	Editing
Formatting	Cover Design
	Formatting
	Upload eBooks to Amazon
	Upload Paperback to Amazon
ADVANCE PACKAGE	**LDP SUPREME PACKAGE**
$1,400	**$1,700**
Typing	Typing
Editing (line editing/content)	Editing (line editing/content)
Cover Design	Cover Design
Formatting	Formatting
Copyright Registration	Copyright Registration
Proofreading	Proofreading
Upload eBooks to Amazon	Set up Amazon Account
Upload Paperback to Amazon	Upload eBooks to Amazon
	Upload Paperback to Amazon
	Advertise on LDP's Amazon and
	Facebook Page

***Other services available upon request.
Additional charges may apply

Lock Down Publications
P.O. Box 944
Stockbridge, GA 30281-9998
Phone: 470 303-9761
Email: lockdownpublications@gmail.com

133

Submission Guideline

Submit the first three chapters of your completed manuscript to ldpsubmissions@gmail.com. In the subject line add **Your Book's Title**. The manuscript must be in a Word Doc file and sent as an attachment. Document should be in Times New Roman, double spaced, and in size 12 font. Also, provide your synopsis and full contact information. If sending multiple submissions, they must each be in a separate email.

Have a story but no way to send it electronically? You can still submit to LDP/Ca$h Presents. Send in the first three chapters, written or typed, of your completed manuscript to:

LDP: Submissions Dept
P.O. Box 944
Stockbridge, GA 30281-9998

DO NOT send original manuscript. Must be a duplicate. Provide your synopsis and a cover letter containing your full contact information.

Thanks for considering LDP and Ca$h Presents.

NEW RELEASES

BLOODLINE OF A SAVAGE 1&2
THESE VICIOUS STREETS 1&2
RELENTLESS GOON
RELENTLESS GOON 2
BY PRINCE A. TAUHID

THE BUTTERFLY MAFIA 1-3
BY FUMIYA PAYNE

A THUG'S STREET PRINCESS 1&2
BY MEESHA

CITY OF SMOKE 2
BY MOLOTTI

STEPPERS 1,2&3
THE REAL BADDIES OF CHI-RAQ
BY KING RIO

THE LANE 1&2
BY KEN-KEN SPENCE

THUG OF SPADES 1&2
LOVE IN THE TRENCHES 2
CORNER BOYS
BY COREY ROBINSON

TIL DEATH 3
BY ARYANNA

THE BIRTH OF A GANGSTER 4
BY DELMONT PLAYER

PRODUCT OF THE STREETS 1&2
BY DEMOND "MONEY" ANDERSON

MARTELL "TROUBLESOME" BOLDEN

NO TIME FOR ERROR
BY KEESE

MONEY HUNGRY DEMONS
BY TRANAY ADAMS

Coming Soon from Lock Down Publications/Ca$h Presents

IF YOU CROSS ME ONCE 6
ANGEL V
By Anthony Fields

IMMA DIE BOUT MINE 5
By Aryanna

A THUGS STREET PRINCESS 3
By Meesha

PRODUCT OF THE STREETS 3
By Demond Money Anderson

CORNER BOYS 2
By Corey Robinson

THE MURDER QUEENS 6&7
By Michael Gallon

CITY OF SMOKE 3
By Molotti

CONFESSIONS OF A DOPE BOY
By Nicholas Lock

THA TAKEOVER
By Keith Chandler

BETRAYAL OF A G 2
By Ray Vinci

CRIME BOSS
By Playa Ray

Available Now

RESTRAINING ORDER 1 & 2
By **CA$H & Coffee**

LOVE KNOWS NO BOUNDARIES 1-3
By **Coffee**

RAISED AS A GOON I, II, III & IV
BRED BY THE SLUMS I, II, III
BLAST FOR ME I & II
ROTTEN TO THE CORE I II III
A BRONX TALE I, II, III
DUFFLE BAG CARTEL I II III IV V VI
HEARTLESS GOON I II III IV V
A SAVAGE DOPEBOY I II
DRUG LORDS I II III
CUTTHROAT MAFIA I II
KING OF THE TRENCHES
By **Ghost**

LAY IT DOWN I & II
LAST OF A DYING BREED I II
BLOOD STAINS OF A SHOTTA I & II III
By **Jamaica**

LOYAL TO THE GAME I II III
LIFE OF SIN I, II III
By **TJ & Jelissa**

IF LOVING HIM IS WRONG…I & II
LOVE ME EVEN WHEN IT HURTS I II III
By **Jelissa**

PUSH IT TO THE LIMIT
By **Bre' Hayes**

CARTEL MONEY 2

MARTELL "TROUBLESOME" BOLDEN

BLOOD OF A BOSS 1-5
SHADOWS OF THE GAME
TRAP BASTARD
By **Askari**

THE STREETS BLEED MURDER 1-3
THE HEART OF A GANGSTA 1-3
By **Jerry Jackson**

WHEN A GOOD GIRL GOES BAD
By **Adrienne**

THE COST OF LOYALTY 1-3
By **Kweli**

BRIDE OF A HUSTLA 1-3
THE FETTI GIRLS 1-3
CORRUPTED BY A GANGSTA 1-4
BLINDED BY HIS LOVE
THE PRICE YOU PAY FOR LOVE 1-3
DOPE GIRL MAGIC 1-3
By **Destiny Skai**

A KINGPIN'S AMBITION
A KINGPIN'S AMBITION II
I MURDER FOR THE DOUGH
By **Ambitious**

TRUE SAVAGE 1-7
DOPE BOY MAGIC 1-3
MIDNIGHT CARTEL 1-3
CITY OF KINGZ 1&2
NIGHTMARE ON SILENT AVE
THE PLUG OF LIL MEXICO 1&2
CLASSIC CITY
By **Chris Green**

CARTEL MONEY 2

A GANGSTER'S REVENGE 1-4
THE BOSS MAN'S DAUGHTERS 1-5
A SAVAGE LOVE 1&2
BAE BELONGS TO ME 1&2
A HUSTLER'S DECEIT 1-3
WHAT BAD BITCHES DO 1-3
SOUL OF A MONSTER 1-3
KILL ZONE
A DOPE BOY'S QUEEN 1-3
TIL DEATH 1-3
IMMA DIE BOUT MINE 1-4
By **Aryanna**

A DOPEBOY'S PRAYER
By **Eddie "Wolf" Lee**

THE KING CARTEL 1-3
By **Frank Gresham**

THESE NIGGAS AIN'T LOYAL 1-3
By **Nikki Tee**

GANGSTA SHYT 1-3
By **CATO**

THE ULTIMATE BETRAYAL
By **Phoenix**

BOSS'N UP 1-3
By **Royal Nicole**

I LOVE YOU TO DEATH
By **Destiny J**

I RIDE FOR MY HITTA
I STILL RIDE FOR MY HITTA
By **Misty Holt**

MARTELL "TROUBLESOME" BOLDEN

LOVE & CHASIN' PAPER
By **Qay Crockett**

TO DIE IN VAIN
SINS OF A HUSTLA
By **ASAD**

BROOKLYN HUSTLAZ
By **Boogsy Morina**

BROOKLYN ON LOCK 1 & 2
By **Sonovia**

GANGSTA CITY
By **Teddy Duke**

A DRUG KING AND HIS DIAMOND 1-3
A DOPEMAN'S RICHES
HER MAN, MINE'S TOO 1&2
CASH MONEY HO'S
THE WIFEY I USED TO BE 1&2
PRETTY GIRLS DO NASTY THINGS
By **Nicole Goosby**

LIPSTICK KILLAH 1-3
CRIME OF PASSION 1-3
FRIEND OR FOE 1-3
By **Mimi**

TRAPHOUSE KING 1-3
KINGPIN KILLAZ 1-3
STREET KINGS 1&2
PAID IN BLOOD 1&2
CARTEL KILLAZ 1-3
DOPE GODS 1&2
By **Hood Rich**

THE STREETS ARE CALLING
By **Duquie Wilson**

CARTEL MONEY 2

STEADY MOBBN' 1-3
THE STREETS STAINED MY SOUL 1-3
By **Marcellus Allen**

WHO SHOT YA 1-3
SON OF A DOPE FIEND 1-4
HEAVEN GOT A GHETTO 1&2
SKI MASK MONEY 1&2
By **Renta**

GORILLAZ IN THE BAY 1-4
TEARS OF A GANGSTA 1/&2
3X KRAZY 1&2
STRAIGHT BEAST MODE 1&2
By **DE'KARI**

TRIGGADALE 1-3
MURDA WAS THE CASE 1-3
By **Elijah R. Freeman**

SLAUGHTER GANG 1-3
RUTHLESS HEART 1-3
By **Willie Slaughter**

GOD BLESS THE TRAPPERS 1-3
THESE SCANDALOUS STREETS 1-3
FEAR MY GANGSTA 1-5
THESE STREETS DON'T LOVE NOBODY 1-2
BURY ME A G 1-5
A GANGSTA'S EMPIRE 1-4
THE DOPEMAN'S BODYGAURD 1&2
THE REALEST KILLAZ 1-3
THE LAST OF THE OGS 1-3
By **Tranay Adams**

MARRIED TO A BOSS 1-3
By **Destiny Skai & Chris Green**

MARTELL "TROUBLESOME" BOLDEN

KINGZ OF THE GAME 1-7
CRIME BOSS 1-3
By **Playa Ray**

FUK SHYT
By **Blakk Diamond**

DON'T F#CK WITH MY HEART 1&2
By **Linnea**

ADDICTED TO THE DRAMA 1-3
IN THE ARM OF HIS BOSS
By **Jamila**

LOYALTY AIN'T PROMISED 1&2
By **Keith Williams**

YAYO 1-4
A SHOOTER'S AMBITION 1&2
BRED IN THE GAME
By **S. Allen**

TRAP GOD 1-3
RICH $AVAGE 1-3
MONEY IN THE GRAVE 1-3
CARTEL MONEY
By **Martell Troublesome Bolden**

FOREVER GANGSTA 1&2
GLOCKS ON SATIN SHEETS 1&2
By **Adrian Dulan**

TOE TAGZ 1-4
LEVELS TO THIS SHYT 1&2
IT'S JUST ME AND YOU
By **Ah'Million**

CARTEL MONEY 2

KINGPIN DREAMS 1-3
RAN OFF ON DA PLUG
By **Paper Boi Rari**

THE STREETS MADE ME 1-3
By **Larry D. Wright**

CONFESSIONS OF A GANGSTA 1-4
CONFESSIONS OF A JACKBOY 1-3
CONFESSIONS OF A HITMAN
By **Nicholas Lock**

I'M NOTHING WITHOUT HIS LOVE
SINS OF A THUG
TO THE THUG I LOVED BEFORE
A GANGSTA SAVED XMAS
IN A HUSTLER I TRUST
By **Monet Dragun**

QUIET MONEY 1-3
THUG LIFE 1-3
EXTENDED CLIP 1&2
A GANGSTA'S PARADISE
By **Trai'Quan**

CAUGHT UP IN THE LIFE 1-3
THE STREETS NEVER LET GO 1-3
By **Robert Baptiste**

NEW TO THE GAME 1-3
MONEY, MURDER & MEMORIES 1-3
By **Malik D. Rice**

CREAM 2-3
THE STREETS WILL TALK
By **Yolanda Moore**

THE STREETS WILL NEVER CLOSE 1-3
By **K'ajji**

MARTELL "TROUBLESOME" BOLDEN

LIFE OF A SAVAGE 1-4
A GANGSTA'S QUR'AN 1-4
MURDA SEASON 1-3
GANGLAND CARTEL 1-3
CHI'RAQ GANGSTAS 1-4
KILLERS ON ELM STREET 1-3
JACK BOYZ N DA BRONX 1-3
A DOPEBOY'S DREAM 1-3
JACK BOYS VS DOPE BOYS 1-3
COKE GIRLZ
COKE BOYS
SOSA GANG 1&2
BRONX SAVAGES
BODYMORE KINGPINS
BLOOD OF A GOON
By **Romell Tukes**

CONCRETE KILLA 1-3
VICIOUS LOYALTY 1-3
By **Kingpen**

THE ULTIMATE SACRIFICE 1-6
KHADIFI
IF YOU CROSS ME ONCE 1-3
ANGEL 1-4
IN THE BLINK OF AN EYE
By **Anthony Fields**

THE LIFE OF A HOOD STAR
By **Ca$h & Rashia Wilson**

NIGHTMARES OF A HUSTLA 1-3
BLOOD AND GAMES 1&2
By **King Dream**

GHOST MOB
By **Stilloan Robinson**

CARTEL MONEY 2

HARD AND RUTHLESS 1&2
MOB TOWN 251
THE BILLIONAIRE BENTLEYS 1-3
REAL G'S MOVE IN SILENCE
By **Von Diesel**

MOB TIES 1-7
SOUL OF A HUSTLER, HEART OF A KILLER 1-3
GORILLAZ IN THE TRENCHES
By **SayNoMore**

BODYMORE MURDERLAND 1-3
THE BIRTH OF A GANGSTER 1-4
By **Delmont Player**

FOR THE LOVE OF A BOSS 1&2
By **C. D. Blue**

KILLA KOUNTY 1-5
By **Khufu**

MOBBED UP 1-4
THE BRICK MAN 1-5
THE COCAINE PRINCESS 1-10
STEPPERS 1-3
SUPER GREMLIN 1-4
By **King Rio**

MONEY GAME 1&2
By **Smoove Dolla**

A GANGSTA'S KARMA 1-4
By **FLAME**

KING OF THE TRENCHES 1-3
By **GHOST & TRANAY ADAMS**

MARTELL "TROUBLESOME" BOLDEN

QUEEN OF THE ZOO 1&2
By **Black Migo**

GRIMEY WAYS 1-3
BETRAYAL OF A G
By **Ray Vinci**

XMAS WITH AN ATL SHOOTER
By **Ca$h & Destiny Skai**

KING KILLA 1&2
By **Vincent "Vitto" Holloway**

BETRAYAL OF A THUG 1&2
By **Fre$h**

THE MURDER QUEENS 1-5
By **Michael Gallon**

FOR THE LOVE OF BLOOD 1-4
By **Jamel Mitchell**

HOOD CONSIGLIERE 1&2
NO TIME FOR ERROR
By **Keese**

PROTÉGÉ OF A LEGEND 1&2
LOVE IN THE TRENCHES 1&2
By **Corey Robinson**

THE PLUG'S RUTHLESS DAUGHTER
By **Tony Daniels**

BORN IN THE GRAVE 1-3
CRIME PAYS
By **Self Made Tay**

MOAN IN MY MOUTH
By **XTASY**

CARTEL MONEY 2

TORN BETWEEN A GANGSTER AND A GENTLEMAN
By **J-BLUNT & Miss Kim**

LOYALTY IS EVERYTHING 1-3
CITY OF SMOKE 1&2
By **Molotti**

HERE TODAY GONE TOMORROW 1&2
By **Fly Rock**

WOMEN LIE MEN LIE 1-4
FIFTY SHADES OF SNOW 1-3
STACK BEFORE YOU SPLURGE
GIRLS FALL LIKE DOMINOES
NAÏVE TO THE STREETS
By **ROY MILLIGAN**

PILLOW PRINCESS
By **S. Hawkins**

THE BUTTERFLY MAFIA 1-3
SALUTE MY SAVAGERY 1&2
By **Fumiya Payne**

THE LANE 1&2
By Ken-Ken Spence

THE PUSSY TRAP 1-5
By **Nene Capri**

DIRTY DNA
By **Blaque**

SANCTIFIED AND HORNY
by **XTASY**

149

BOOKS BY LDP'S CEO, CA$H

TRUST IN NO MAN
TRUST IN NO MAN 2
TRUST IN NO MAN 3
BONDED BY BLOOD
SHORTY GOT A THUG
THUGS CRY
THUGS CRY 2
THUGS CRY 3
TRUST NO BITCH
TRUST NO BITCH 2
TRUST NO BITCH 3
TIL MY CASKET DROPS
RESTRAINING ORDER
RESTRAINING ORDER 2
IN LOVE WITH A CONVICT
LIFE OF A HOOD STAR
XMAS WITH AN ATL SHOOTER